THE SECT

Book 1, The Resistance Files

About the Author

Eliza Green tried her hand at fashion designing, massage, painting, and even ghost hunting, before finding her love of writing. She often wonders if her desire to change the ending of a particular glittery vampire story steered her in that direction (it did). After earning her degree in marketing, Eliza went on to work in everything but marketing, but swears she uses it in everyday life, or so she tells her bank manager.

Born and raised in Dublin, Ireland, she lives there with her sci-fi loving, evil genius best friend. When not working on her next amazing science fiction adventure, you can find her reading, indulging in new food at an amazing restaurant or simply singing along to something with a half decent beat.

For a list of all available books, check out:

www.elizagreenbooks.com/books

BOOK 1 IN THE RESISTANCE FILES

THE SECT

ELIZA GREEN

Copyright © 2021 Eliza Green

The moral right of the author has been asserted in accordance with the Copyright, Designs and Patents Act 1988.
All rights reserved. No part of this publication may be reproduced, stored in a retrieval system, or transmitted, in any form or by any means, without the prior written permission of the author, nor be otherwise circulated in any form of binding or cover other than that in which it is published and without a similar condition being imposed on the subsequent purchaser.
All characters in this publication are fictitious and any resemblance to real persons, living or dead, is purely coincidental.

ISBN: 9798848184075

Copy Editor: Sara Litchfield
Cover: GetCovers

*Dedicated to good friends.
Let nothing come between them.*

1

Anya

Anya covered her ears just as Jason's nasal singing reached full-blown pitch. She'd never hated his guts so much.

'I wish he was dead.'

'Anya!' her mother, Grace, chided. 'What a terrible thing to say about your brother.'

'He's not my brother.'

She'd disowned him after he'd stolen her favorite toy and taken it apart, so he could learn how to become a Neer. That's what the Corp called Engineers. Anya had another name for him: an arrogant ass who should mind his own business and keep out of her room. Who would the next victim of his sick experiments be—her Synth friend?

'I'm just glad Cynthia isn't here to see his wanton destruction of her close cousin.'

Her father, Evan, laughed. 'Your toy dog has

been sitting in a box for three years gathering dust. You stopped playing with it.'

Evan's mockery twisted her heart. Hard. 'Just because I'm not playing with it now doesn't mean I'm done with it. Remington belonged to me. Jason had no right to take him.'

Her mother bent down to her level, in that way she used to when Anya was little. She smelled like the peppery freesias that filled the window boxes outside their apartment windows. But mixed with Jason's oil and grease, the combination made her stomach swirl.

'Look, Anya, you're sixteen and not a kid anymore,' said Grace. 'Toys are for kids and Jason has a real shot at getting picked for Neer training next year. He needs to practice.'

It was just like her mother to take Jason's side.

'Grace,'—that's what she would refer to her as from now on—'according to the Corp's handbook, it's illegal for someone to enter another person's space without their permission. They could be tried and killed for their crime.'

That's what Cynthia had taught her. And she should know. She had the rule book stored in her memory banks.

Her mother scowled and shook her arm. 'Did your Synth friend teach you that?' She turned to the other half of Anya's parental control. 'Evan, see what *that Synth* is teaching our child?'

Her words squeezed Anya's heart. 'Her name is Cynthia! And she's my best friend. Don't you want me to have a friend?'

Sometimes she wondered about her mother's motives.

Grace gazed at her with nauseating pity in her eyes. 'Of course you should have friends. But you don't hang out with anyone else except that Synth girl. Why can't you pick a normal friend for a change—one that doesn't teach you to be fearful of the Corp?'

She didn't fear the Corp. The rules were there to protect everyone in the areas that had been chosen as colonies, and within the cities that had been turned into Sects. United America had more European immigrants than natives. Protection was necessary to keep the Sect dwellers safe from the Exiled and the Synths safe from the less tolerant Sect dwellers living in the lower zones.

Intolerant people like her mother.

Anya took a deep breath to control the temper simmering close to her surface.

Invoking a partial calm, she said, 'Grace, Evan, I'll thank you to let me choose my own friends. And in the future, if you permit that... that... idiot in there to take anything else of mine, I will have no choice but to choose a skill that guarantees you'll never see me again.'

Her parents' eyes widened—good. But only for a second—bad. She'd used this threat too many times. There were five skills in the San Francisco Sect, but only the Tech role demanded true isolation. Having zero skills also guaranteed separation. To live in the Sects, people had to be of some value to the Corp.

The Sect

The Moles were the lowest skilled workers and lived in the outermost zone of the San Francisco Sect. It was the poorest area and closest to the exit. The people there fixed the utilities in the Sect and were always the hungriest. A lot of stealing went on there.

The Neers designed and built the military bases. They were pretty well off and many Synths, upon reaching their second life cycle, occupied this group.

The Sols, or Soldiers, worked for the military base that overlooked the San Fran Sect. They protected the Sect from the Exiled who lived outside the Sect's high walls. But the recruits were quick to temper, mostly due to the emotion blockers they received and the muscle-enhancing injections that made them stronger.

The Techs were highly respected and segregated from the population, mainly because of their ability to open anything in the city. The Corp didn't trust them to live among the population, because of the risk they might be kidnapped and ransomed by the Moles or the Exiled.

Lastly, the Earthers provided food for this Sect, and were the most pragmatic about the segregated life these five particular skills enforced upon the Corp's people.

Her parents were natural Earthers, and Jason's penchant for electronics could pitch him into a job with the Neers, one up from the Earthers and better paid. But Anya had no skills, no interest in any of the predetermined job roles—and her parents knew it. She would probably be forced to learn hydroponics and work alongside them for the rest of her life. The thought of being an Earther like them made her sick.

A fresh look of pity flashed across her parents' faces. Anya tensed up. With a grunt, she stormed out of the tiny living room and upstairs to her box-sized bedroom. At least she had her own room. Thank you, puberty.

She slammed the door. It shuddered in the frame. *Damn, that felt good.*

A tingle of delight ran up her spine when Grace's warning followed. 'Don't slam the door!'

Too late.

Their golden child, Jason, was the only one worth their time and effort. His Neer wages would shift the family out of their average-income existence. He could do no wrong.

Anya threw herself onto the bed with a huff, and buried her head deep under her pillow. She had to find a way out of her predetermined life with the Earthers. Their level-headedness drove her mad. Always with an answer for everything. Nothing ever bothered them. Everyone deserved a chance—except Synths, according to her mother. Their nauseating empathy for all people —emphasis on *people*—made her skin crawl.

She flung the pillow to the floor and flipped onto her back. With another huff, Anya lifted her hand, holding it up against a background of primrose yellow —the color of her wall. She called the only person that she could bear to talk to these days.

'Call Cynthia,' she said.

A holographic screen the size of her hand was displayed before her, enabled by the chip buried beneath her skin.

The connection rang and rang, then it connected. Anya breathed out a sigh of relief when a familiar face appeared. The blonde-haired sixteen-year-old on her screen was the best friend Anya could hope for.

'You look like you've been told you're grounded,' Cynthia said with a frown.

'Feels like it. This place is like a damn prison.'

Cynthia tilted her head slightly. 'What can I do to cheer you up?'

Any distraction would do. 'Tell me about your day.'

Cynthia looked off to the side, then looked back. 'Well, let's see. It's Saturday morning, so I got up and got dressed. Then I had breakfast, went for a jog, came back and had a shower. Then I got a call from you.'

Anya smiled at her attempt. Seeing her friend on screen wasn't enough. This tiny house was making her skin feel tight.

'Wanna meet for a chat?'

Cynthia hesitated. 'I thought you were grounded.'

'No, you thought I *looked* grounded. I'm just in a rotten mood.'

'Lemme guess... Jason.'

'Who else? He's getting worse.' Anya rolled her eyes. 'Our usual spot?'

Cynthia smiled and nodded. 'See you in twenty.'

2

Anya

Anya arrived at Golden Gate Fields, a former horse racing destination hugging the edge of the Bay, now an open visitors' park.

She climbed the steps to the elevated viewing area offering a perfect view of Pier 45, Fisherman's Wharf and Alcatraz Island. Anya pressed her chip to the viewing scope to activate it. She looked down the scope at Pier 45, seeing the usual waterside activity from the Sols. The military base set into the San Bruno Mountain often used the tech-free Alcatraz for Sol training purposes. A rail bridge connected the mainland to the island. She had rarely seen the one-track bridge not in use.

She sat down on the bench near the scope and breathed in the fresh air. She closed her eyes and concentrated on the feel of the sea wind on her face.

The sound of chatting forced her eyes open. Groups of people walked the path below the viewing platform. Some she recognized as Synths. Not many could tell the difference between the organic, humanlike machines and actual humans, but Anya could. Sometimes their fingers danced on occasion, like they were conducting at a concert. Cynthia had explained it was a twitch, something that happened when the brain stem lost connection to the body for a split second. Nothing to worry about, she'd added. So Anya didn't.

She spotted her friend before she arrived. Cynthia's long, blonde, braided hair reached the middle of her back. It bobbed as she ran. She was wearing the standard training gear for school. Anya hated her slate-gray uniform, but Cynthia loved how comfortable it felt against her skin.

Her friend loved to run, and this would be her second one today. It wasn't a Synth thing but a Cynthia thing. Cynthia had narrowed down her second-life-cycle skill choices to either Sol or Earther. Apparently, running would give her an early head start on the requirement to be fit for either profession. Although, Anya was sure the latter was just a sympathy pick by Cynthia, to prove to Anya that Earthers mattered as a career choice.

Cynthia jogged up the steps and crumpled next to Anya on the bench. Her breaths came short and fast. Synths had lungs like regular people. Except theirs were part organic, part machine. The machine part talked to the machine brain, which was more network and connections than gray matter.

Anya envied her friend. She had the whole world at her feet. She could do anything, be anything.

She set her shoulders back and hid her jealousy behind a false confidence.

A huffing and puffing Cynthia nudged her with her elbow. 'Hey, weirdo.'

Anya managed a smile. 'Hey.'

She watched the train run along the track between Pier 45 and the island. In the Bay, automated, floating containers pulled into numbered docks, and others, similarly marked with the Corp brand, floated out. Trade with the other Sects.

'Lots of activity today,' said Cynthia. 'I hear they've got new recruits for the Sols, but they haven't received their emotion blockers or muscle injections yet. They're taking them out to the island for the next part.'

The muscle-enhancing injections designed to make the Sols stronger turned them berserk for a while. It was safer to have them off the mainland while treatments were being administered for everyone's safety, including the Sols'.

'Do you think you might become a Sol?' asked Anya.

She looked at her friend. She had the physique for it. Plus she loved to exercise.

Cynthia gazed at the water. 'Not sure yet. I still have a while before my first life cycle completes.'

When Cynthia turned seventeen, she would enter her second life cycle. Her development would be paused for five years while she completed her training. At that point, she would be developed further, physically or mentally, depending on which trade she showed the highest aptitude for.

Anya hugged herself as she turned back to the rail connection. The train had reached the island and small flecks resembling humans were disembarking.

'I don't know if I could be a Sol,' she said. 'They seem so... cold.'

It wasn't just Synths who became ice kings and queens after treatment. Humans did too.

'Yeah, I believe it's due to the emotion blockers they receive. They mess with the brain's chemistry.' Cynthia touched Anya's hand. 'But that wouldn't happen to me. I wouldn't need injections or blockers. I would just receive an upgrade.'

'To change your personality parameters.'

'Only minor tweaks. I would still be me. They can't erase that.'

Anya squeezed her hand and smiled. Maybe this was why she didn't have human friends. If one of them became a Sol and turned into a colder version of themselves, would she want them as a friend anymore? At least with Cynthia, there would be no need for crazy changes to her personality.

She hoped.

'So, what did Jason do now?' Cynthia asked, reclaiming her hand and setting both on her lap.

The fight seemed petty now that Anya was away from the claustrophobic box they called home. It was so small she could have swung a cat in it—if pets were permitted in the Sect.

'He took something that didn't belong to him.'

'Seems like that's all he does these days.'

That wasn't true. 'It wasn't that bad.'

'But he's always in your stuff, right?'

No, he wasn't. 'This is the first time he's taken anything.'

Cynthia nodded. 'But it was valuable, no?'

'Not really.' Anya sighed. 'I hadn't played with the toy for a few years.'

The edge of Cynthia's mouth turned up. 'So, Jason took something that you didn't play with anymore so he could do what... destroy it?'

'No, he has the potential to be a Neer.' She shrugged. 'He needed something to practice on, I guess.'

'An engineer? Wow.' Cynthia widened her eyes. 'That's a step up from an Earther. More pay for a start.'

Anya smiled and shook her head. She knew what Cynthia was doing. 'Okay, I get it. What he did wasn't all that bad and I'm blowing it out of proportion.'

Her friend snorted. 'I'd say.'

'Have you ever considered being a Psych?'

'Not a recognized job in this Sect, so no.'

Psychologists existed in other Sects, but not in this one. The Corp didn't regard their skill set as useful enough to be included in the main five. Psychs with a secondary skill like Utility or Gardening had been assigned to those main areas. Any without a useful skill had been banished to the outside as an Exile. It was what Anya risked if she didn't pick a skill.

She changed the subject. 'So, how's your training coming along?'

Cynthia's mouth turned down. 'Okay, I suppose. I'm following the training schedule to see if I have what it takes to be a Sol, but it feels like I'm getting nowhere. I have limited information on what the real test will be like.'

'Maybe your next software upgrade will give you more information.'

'I'd prefer a hardware update.'

Synths received monthly software upgrades to fix bugs and improve information flow to the machine parts of the brain and body, as well as to add new knowledge. Hardware updates were different, in that they made a Synth stronger or more resilient, or more empathetic, or more tech minded. But that wouldn't come until after Cynthia completed her first life cycle.

Anya looked over at Pier 45. There was new activity. She stepped up to the scope once more and zoomed in on the location. A large vehicle had pulled up with the word CorpTech emblazoned on the side. Several male and female teenagers got out, dressed in gray tracksuits similar to the one Cynthia wore. They looked nervous, excited.

A man in uniform said something to them and they lined up, like the pre-soldiers they were. He shouted something she couldn't hear. They nodded, eyes forward, eager anticipation lodged in them. Then he must have ordered them to move, because they filed onto the monorail that would take them from the pier to the island.

Anya wished she had an interest in something. But one thing was clear: She didn't want to be a Sol. The simple fact that she'd snuck out of the house without telling anyone only proved she didn't take direction well. And she'd need that in spades to become a soldier.

Cynthia on the other hand was calm, and could handle any situation.

The parks were designated as communal spaces, meaning they were open to all skill types. The time before lunch was always a busy one. It marked the end of the morning shift for the Moles, who had been up since dawn fixing the Sect's broken sinks and communal drains. It was a dirty job with long hours, but someone had to do it. The Synths might have been the natural choice at one point, but the Corp regarded them as too valuable a commodity to descend below the city streets or live in the poorest zone.

A man dressed in greasy overalls walked past. He did a double take at Cynthia lounging on the bench, taking in the sun, and stopped. When he walked up the steps, Anya tensed and sat back down. Her heart pounded thickly. He was a Mole, the least tolerable of the skilled workers.

The Mole eyed Cynthia. 'You're one of them. A Synth, aren't you?'

Cynthia sat up straight, looking like a rabbit

caught in headlights. 'I—I'm just with my friend.'

He turned his hot gaze on Anya and gave her a sharp nod. 'You watch what you tell these things, little girl. Who knows what the Corp is learning from them come upgrade time?'

Anya's cheeks bloomed with embarrassment. She went to tell him to mind his own business, but her throat tightened and caught the words.

The man sneered at her and raked his gaze over Cynthia, like she was a piece of filth. A blaze of anger tightened Anya's chest. She balled her fists.

'Leave them alone,' said a woman who was passing by.

The Mole broke off his stare, then turned and trotted down the steps.

'Synth lover,' he muttered to the woman as he walked off.

The woman stopped. 'You two okay?'

Anya stood up, feeling a little shaky. 'Yeah. He was just a Mole.'

It's what Jason would have said if he'd been here.

'Moles have no business being in this park,' said the woman, her head turned in the direction the man was walking.

Anya rolled her eyes. 'Tell me about it.'

'Stop it,' Cynthia hissed at Anya.

The woman walked off, leaving Anya with one angry Synth.

'Why do you have to say that stuff?'

Anya frowned. 'About what?'

'About Moles. That woman, she's a snob.'

Anya sat back down. 'Well, maybe I'm one, too, because I don't like Moles who speak to my friend like that.'

'Don't you get it? You agreeing with that woman is the same as agreeing that differences matter. That Synths are different.'

'That's not what I meant...'

'It is, and you know it.'

Truth was, Anya was angry at herself for not sticking up for Cynthia, that it had taken a stranger to say what she should have. But she hated rocking the boat anywhere else but at home. That's why she'd most likely end up an Earther while Cynthia would be someone amazing.

'Moles think Synths are dangerous, unpredictable,' said Anya.

Jason had told her that. And it was partly why she hated her brother—because he believed it too.

Cynthia shook her head. 'I'm not programmed to hate. I can't.'

'I know, that's why I said that about the Moles. All they do is hate. Point out differences. I was just defending you...'

Cynthia stood and brushed imaginary dirt off her impeccable clothes. 'I've got to go. Chat to you later.'

She jogged down the steps and along the path. Anya watched her leave. Next time she'd be brave, and tell the Mole exactly what she thought of him.

The Sect

She sat there a moment longer, vowing to never become one of them.

3

Cynthia

She wished it didn't bother her, but it was the sixth insult Cynthia had received that month. Always from the Moles. And she'd noticed a few Sols—some Synths—had been near to the viewing platform and had not said anything. In some ways, that was worse.

She kept her stride even along the track leading out of the park, wishing there were a way she could hide what she was. Synths were indistinguishable from humans, except for the connection site at the back of their heads that facilitated their receipt of software upgrades. But her blonde hair hid all that. And the cap she wore helped. So, how had the Mole known?

Her fingers danced as she ran—a side effect from her last upgrade. A glitch that interrupted the signal from brain to body. But only a few noticed the anomaly enough to mention it.

Always Moles.

What was so different about Zone Six where

The Sect

Moles lived compared to Zones Two to Five housing the other skilled workers? What was being taught in their neighborhood for them to hate Synths so much?

The irony? Moles had nothing to worry about. Cynthia had been programmed with empathy and higher learning. If anyone was destined to turn violent, it wouldn't be her.

Cynthia exited the gate and pounded the road hard with an even stride. Her breath thickened, thanks to her part-organic-part-machine Synth lungs. She and other Synths had been designed in this way to blend in and become useful members of society. Their destiny was to enhance the quality of life for those humans living in the Sect. People accepted Synths.

Except for the Moles, it seemed.

She arrived at the monorail and took the steps two at a time to the train platform, elevated high above the city. Her hands twitched again. She twisted them together.

A light-blue message flashed across her hand. *Call your mother.*

Cynthia dialed the number she knew off by heart.

'Hey,' she said when her mother's face appeared.

Her mother frowned. 'Where are you?'

'About to get on the train. Why?'

'I received a notice that your software upgrade is later today, 5pm. Did you forget?'

Cynthia blushed and looked around as her human mother's voice carried across the packed platform. She checked for more Moles that would use this detail as an excuse to attack her verbally. But those around her had their heads dipped low, too busy reading news articles on their hands to follow her conversation.

She breathed out a soft sigh and lowered her voice. 'I'll be there. I haven't forgotten.'

'Will you be home first?'

'In a couple of hours. I've got some prep stuff to do first—at the Station.'

It was a lie, but on her upgrade days her mother was more attentive than she could handle. During these overprotective moments, Cynthia wished to be left alone. Her parents were human Earthers, assigned to her at her creation, designed to help her understand humanity and to help her blend in with society.

Except for their annoying over protectiveness, Cynthia had no issues with them. After she completed her first life cycle they would no longer be her parents. Cynthia would become part of the Corp's finely tuned machine, another cog ready to turn their industry wheel. Anya had voiced her objection often over Cynthia's predetermined role in life, but Cynthia had no problem with it. To serve the Corp was her ultimate goal.

She was made for it. Literally.

'I'll talk to you later,' she said to her mother.

'Okay, honey. See you at home.'

The train pulled into the station just as Cynthia clicked off. She readjusted her cap, turned up her collar, and climbed on board.

The train left Zone One, a communal place where the elite lived but all the skills mingled. It was where most of the general trade happened. It was also the location of the Base. The residential zones, Two to Six, were separated by tall walls and entry gates, accessible only by vehicles operating under the Base's—meaning the Corp's—command. Her father said the separation was because the different skills kept different hours, and it was better if workers in the same zone lived together. But to Cynthia, the rules meant a deeper segregation between the skills, at the Corp's behest.

The train made its usual stops, finally reaching the edge of Zone One. From there, the train would enter Zones Two through to Six. She had never been farther than Five, the Earthers' zone, where she and Anya lived.

The train slipped over the rooftops and the gray concrete walls keeping the residential areas separate. The only way to access them was by train, or by vehicles commissioned by the Base, with special access to the gates between them. The Sect was like a prison in a way.

The train reached the last stop in Zone Five. Many got off and seats became free. Cynthia gripped the edge of her seat and closed her eyes. The doors shut and the train moved off. She opened her eyes, releasing some of her nerves on the next breath.

She didn't venture far inside the last zone... just to the next stop.

When the train arrived at the platform for Six-internal-1, Cynthia hurried off the train and jogged down the steps to street level.

The first thing she noticed in the stairwell was the smell of burning carbon. It infiltrated the air around her, squeezed the goodness out of it. She held her breath, limiting its effects on her lungs, pushing past wheezing humans, who perhaps had become too used to the dirty air. They shot her equally dirty looks when she breathed in and out, unhindered. None of them commented on it though.

That made a nice change.

The bright sunshine pinched her eyes the second she exited the darkened train station. A stench of rotting food caught her unawares and forced her to peg her nose. She spotted piles of garbage lined up outside the station, as if it were a collection point. She increased her step, keen to get past the worst of it.

This zone had a different aroma to that of the Earthers. Five smelled of earth and structure. In Six, it was chaos and instability. Cynthia released her nose and sniffed her wrist, catching a waft of vanilla there. It gave her a momentary break from the harsher notes in the atmosphere.

Her heart pounded in her chest at being here, surrounded by Moles. It was a risky move, but her repeated bad experience with them had prodded her curiosity. She needed to know why the Moles hated her so much.

The streets she walked were stained with oil and grease, like they hadn't been cleaned for some time. Cynthia walked at the Moles' slower pace, hunching over, wheezing, hoping to blend in. Sols dressed in black gear—more visible than in Five—marched the street, keeping an eye on the residents. They looked to be on their usual knife edge, like they might take someone down at a moment's notice. Sols were vicious, strong, bred to be soldiers of the Corp. Cynthia kept her head down as she passed by a group of them who were harassing a resident.

In the near distance, she could see the giant wall separating this Sect from the next one. In the space between lived the Exiled; neither part of this Sect nor the next. She looked up at the large, black and gray structure. If anyone wanted inside the Sect, it wouldn't be over the top. The rumor was, the closer the zone to the wall, the more likely those in it would be Exiled.

Several people knocked into her as they passed. Space inside the Sect was tight, but it appeared to be at its tightest in Six.

Cynthia stayed on her path, keen to keep close to the train in case she had to leave fast. The farther she ventured from the station, the more holographic posters appeared. Some called residents to a group meeting. Others questioned Synths having equal rights to humans. A group of Sols turned into the same road as her. The second they did the posters vanished.

Clever. The posters must dissipate if they picked up Sol chips in the area.

Dangerous. What worried her was the propaganda being peddled behind the Sols' backs. Behind the Corp's back. Allowed to spread and fester as rumors and blame.

As soon as the posters flickered back on, Cynthia zoomed in on one. The image of two smiling people, one with a red X through them, sent a deep chill through her.

Human and Synth.

If the Moles could hide their propaganda this easily from the Sols, they could probably make Cynthia disappear.

She backtracked to the station and boarded the next train back to Five. Four minutes later and safely inside the Earthers' domain, she looked up at the separator between it and Six. The wall was tall, but only a third the height of the outer one. She'd never thought about the Moles before or the zone next to hers, but seeing what was going on there... it was all she could think about now. She'd heard Mole activity was going unchecked. Did the Corp know about it?

She walked home, needing to see a friendly face, wishing her upgrade later that day would give her less empathy and more bravery. Based on what she'd seen, becoming a Sol was looking her best choice to protect herself.

4

Quintus

This was not what Quintus had been designed for. The Corp had created him out of a source code, a compiler and an executable file, and given him sentient thought. He could do more than run security analysis or monitor traffic usage, depending on the given day. But his limitations had come after an accident that hadn't been his fault. The Corp had made his read and limited write —but not edit— functionality no more world changing than the sink-fixing Moles.

His connections tingled, as he sensed the latest upgrade get rolled out to the Station for the Synth program. A program he had helped to design. A program he no longer controlled.

Quintus walked the perimeter of his banal room construct, created inside the program where he lived, tethered to the outside world via a single communication feed the Techs used when they needed his help. Which wasn't often enough. Apparently he'd done his job of designing this Sect's systems too well. His role was as defunct as his editing capabilities.

Now, his reality was a bright, white room, with important code that dripped down the wall and disappeared into the floor. Code he couldn't interact with, only watch.

His private domain. His personal hell.

Agatha had given him physical representation on one condition: He must accept the confines of his room without complaint. Sometimes the firewall would glitch and show him the hidden parameters of his one-room reality. But then the firewall would strengthen, and block access to the next room where edit access could be enabled. He sat in silence too often, until one of the Techs graciously called upon him to help.

Two voices—Techs—boomed overhead. The on-duty men were in mid conversation. Not for the first time, one of them had leaned on the console by mistake, activating the comms.

'Agatha's busting my ass again.'

Agatha, the hardnosed commander of the military base they were in. Quintus recognized the speaker as Shawn, one of the senior Techs.

'So? Do some work then. She's only on your case because you don't turn in your reports on time.'

Leo. A stickler for following rules. His family came from a military background. How disappointed they must have been when their only son chose to become a Tech, not a Sol.

Shawn's voice lifted. 'Who has time for that?'

The Sect

'You should take your job more seriously, you know.'

'Yeah, yeah. When I'm asked to do more than babysit this turd then I will.'

'Who are you talking about?'

'The sentient.' Quintus imagined him shrugging. 'Who else? Agatha doesn't want that drama queen ever getting out.'

Quintus seethed at hearing that. It had been a damn accident, one Agatha would make him pay for over and over. And he was no drama queen. So he'd been making a fuss over his incarceration. What intelligent AI wouldn't?

'Look, man—'

The communication cut out suddenly. Shawn must have leaned against the console to deactivate the comms.

Quintus paced his tight space. It felt more claustrophobic than usual. The hours and days dragged on while he waited for someone to call on him. Sometimes he wished the Corp hadn't made him sentient. Perhaps then he wouldn't care about being stuck inside a reality of someone else's making. Perhaps he would be happy being put in his box, because he wouldn't be aware of it.

Quintus folded himself on the floor with a huff and watched the code streaming down the wall. Something caught his eye, a new change. He stood up and walked over to the wall, stretching his hand out to touch the stream. The action brightened his skin and he read the information off the back of his hand.

This code was something he hadn't seen before. It appeared to be part of the recent software upgrade for the Synths. Yes, he had designed them, but the Techs had been handling their upgrades since the accident. What did this code change?

His curiosity about the Synths had not altered. How was the Corp evolving them?

Quintus moved over to a clear wall without code and activated the console there. It allowed him to change some detail of his confines—wall and floor color from monochrome to a different shade of monochrome, add basic furniture, that sort of thing. But there was also read-write access to the systems Shawn had him check on a daily basis. He checked exploits, attempts at hacking—although the residents in the Sect were oddly compliant—and any systems with critical warnings that might be running out of space. His read-write access gave him the ability to check most stuff and automate certain work, as well as change the names of files. Nothing more.

A gross waste of sentient intelligence.

From the console, he ran a new simulation of the full program with the new code, and compared it against the old, to see what had changed this time.

One line of code gave him pause: a physical alteration to the biological make-up of the Synths that were a year out from the end of their first life cycle. He closed his eyes and processed the information. It all made sense, except for the part that would soon give the

Synths the ability to reproduce. That hadn't been part of the original design. The change intrigued him.

Quintus opened his eyes. He widened them in surprise at seeing another piece of code. This one facilitated a change in the behavioral parameters of the Synths. Nothing alarming in itself, but it appeared to add a new voice trigger that would override the basic command functions. He filed that one away under "to be investigated".

A gruff voice came over the comms system. 'Quintus, can you run diagnostics on security?'

It was Shawn.

The Techs feared him and what he could do. Yes, he was locked up and under control, but Quintus had been programmed with curiosity. In his mind, it was more dangerous *not* to explore.

He replied to Shawn, 'I could do that, or you could let me look at the recent software upgrade. I'm worried there could be a potential conflict issue with it.'

'No can do, man,' said Shawn. His nasal voice grated on Quintus' nerves. 'Agatha doesn't want you working on anything to do with upgrades.'

Quintus pushed the young Tech. 'Did you account for the previous upgrade when you applied changes to the behavioral parameters?'

'Of course we did,' scoffed Shawn. 'We're not idiots, you know.'

That was debatable.

'I would like to speak to Agatha.'

'Sure, sure. First, the security diagnostics. Then

Agatha wants you to check traffic volume. Things are moving a little sluggishly up here.'

'I can do more than that.'

'I know, man... but rules.'

He imagined the tech shrugging. Rules were meant to be broken.

'Tell Agatha I want to speak with her. It's urgent.'

'Keep your pants on... Now I'm under time pressure here. I need you to help me out. The diagnostics?'

Quintus sighed. 'Sure.'

Perhaps he would try again later, when Shawn had calmed down.

With a sigh, he activated his console again and wrote new code to automate the checks, then another set of code to add comments. He wasn't needed for this work, but Agatha insisted he play some role to, in her words, stave off boredom. A necessary evil of having to side-line the talents of sentient beings, he supposed.

He programmed a white, plastic chair. It shimmered in the space before him. He sat down on it, arms folded, and watched the work he'd done diligently for the last year run on autopilot. Quintus didn't know why he'd chosen today of all days to automate it. Maybe he'd thought if he showed he could play by the rules, Agatha might give him more freedom. But after what Shawn had just said, that was unlikely to ever happen.

He stood up and wandered over to the access

panel once more. There, he isolated Agatha's terminal in her office and sent a special message through the reporting function.

Stop ignoring me. We need to talk.

If he couldn't speak to her directly, there were other ways to get her attention.

With a smile, Quintus sat back down and waited.

5

Cynthia

Cynthia stood on the footpath across from the Station and looked up at the tall building, set in the middle of Zone One. It calmed her racing heart to be in the middle of Sect activity, as far away from the oppressive and dirty Zone Six as possible. Her experience in the Moles' sector had left her feeling weird, vulnerable. A quick visit home and a nervous mother had sent her off for another run.

The blackened glass exterior set the Station apart from other structures in the Sect, giving it an authoritative feel. This was where she'd been born, or created, five years ago. It was the birthplace of all the Synths. It was also where she received her monthly upgrades, via special rooms that enabled her to connect to the system.

There was no hiding what she was here. Humans didn't visit the Station for any reason—except maybe the Techs to do maintenance work. But even then, their work didn't always require them to be on site. Most of the work could be done remotely from the Base.

Cynthia hesitated. The second she headed for the building people would know what she was. She'd never hated her Synth status before, but at times she loved being mistaken for human. Anya talked to her like she was no different to Jason, or one of the other human kids at school. Her friend never backed down from any challenge Cynthia might set her. She was supportive when the situation called for it.

This morning in the park had been the exception. Cynthia had sensed fear from her friend, as well as her hesitation to speak up. Her unplanned visit to Zone Six afterwards hadn't widened the gap between Synths and humans. It had already been there, long before the Mole in the park had targeted her.

Taking a deep breath, she checked the way was clear, and jogged across the road. Three Sols marched along the edge of the street. Their pounding feet matched the rhythm of her heart. They looked up at her momentarily as they passed. Many Synths went on to become Sols, so the negativity wasn't as great among them as it was among the Moles. She tipped her chin at one and, with a nervous breath, pushed against the revolving door of the Station. The chilly interior of the Station's white-tiled lobby replaced the mild, autumn air.

Clean, crisp, purified air.

Between her and the real business of the Station

sat a row of security terminals. Beyond that, a large, central staircase leading to the next floor, then two staircases—one left and one right—that turned back to reach a new floor.

Thirteen months remained of her first life cycle. At that point, she would be freed from her parents' care and placed in a new home with the Corp. Anya got angry often when Cynthia brought up the issue of her life cycle ending soon. She didn't blame her friend. She was just worried. Cynthia had no clue either what would happen during the hardware upgrade—whether it would change her, or whether she'd even remember her best friend. Whatever the procedure, a deeper connection existed between her and Anya that she was sure no upgrade could erase.

She approached the row of terminals blocking the way forward. Stepping up to one, she scanned her hand on the screen. It flashed green and the barrier opened to let her pass.

Cynthia knew the way from here. Up the three flights of stairs to the third floor. Last room on the right—room eight. It was always the same. The Corp liked routine, familiarity, efficiency, and no more so than for its Synths. She would need all three in spades when she entered her second life cycle. Might as well get used to it now.

She jogged up the stairs, ignoring the lift that would get her there quicker. The exercise helped to bleed her stress out before an upgrade. Yeah, Synths carried stress too. Hers was mostly to do with the prejudice against her kind; today's stress had to do with the extent to which that prejudice went unchecked in Six. But once a month, she could be herself for a short while, without fear of being singled out.

The third floor was quiet when she arrived on it, the corridor housing her upload room empty of Synths. She liked to arrive several minutes before her allotted upgrade time. It gave her a moment to herself.

Walking past the rooms, Cynthia listened out, hearing the familiar, buzzing sounds of various uploads in process. She stopped outside her room, removed her cap and leaned against the wall. A red light above the door brightened the wall around it. After a few minutes, movement inside sounded and the light flicked over to green. The door opened and Synths of a similar age to her filed out. They were chatting, laughing, joking. Cynthia flashed a closed smile at one girl as she passed. The first life cycle would soon be over for the girl; would she remember how to have fun?

The bright, white room emptied and Cynthia entered it. Set into the longer walls were four pods, two on each one. She stepped inside the pod designated to her and lifted her braid up. A metal arm shot down from the ceiling and dangled there. Cynthia tugged it closer and attached its node to her connection point at the back of her head. Three more Synths entered and took the remaining pods.

The upload started and made her feel lightheaded. Her fingers played out a nonsensical tune. She leaned back and closed her eyes, relishing the time to think, hoping the upload would fix the twitch in her hands.

A warm feeling flowed through her, making her feel weirdly connected to the machine, like it was home for her. She thought of Anya, her friend of the last three years, who stuck up for her, and wasn't usually afraid to say what was on her mind. Kids of Moles attended the same school as them. As the upgrade fed over the network connection, she worried the adults were using their sons and daughters to spread the same propaganda in her school.

Cynthia hoped Anya wasn't being drawn in by the same lies.

The upload made her scalp itchy. A momentary loss of connection jerked her arm up, before it reconnected, and loosened its control of the machine components in her arm. Cynthia flexed her hand. The twitch was gone. One less thing to worry about.

But her doubts went further than a little twitch. What if her second life cycle set her further apart from society? She was permitted no contact with second-life-cycle Synths; she could ask nobody about what life was like on the other side. No manual to study the experience of others either. When the time came, the Corp would drop her into the water and expect her to swim.

The tingling lessened after nine minutes and the machine powered down. Cynthia heard a click next to her ear. She reached back and detached the extended arm from her connection point, then pushed it toward the ceiling. The arm went the rest of the way and a panel closed over it.

She stepped out of the pod and stretched out her body, feeling oddly good. It felt like she'd been injected with a positive mood stimulator. There must have been an update to her personality parameters.

Flexing her hand one more time, she left the room, passing by the next group of upgrade recipients. She smiled at them. Couldn't help it. It must be the mood stimulator. She now understood why the Synths before her had been in such a good mood.

Back in the lobby, Cynthia spotted a group of Sol Synths—three young men—enter the Station. They wore the hardened black body armor of the Sols, but that wasn't how Cynthia recognized them. They had a more muscular physique than the humans, and a colder look in their eyes.

They must be here for their upgrade. Second-life-cycle Synths received their upgrades on the ninth floor, away from the ordinary folks.

When her time came, she hoped her upgrades would preserve her identity and allow her to stay friends with Anya. But given the coldness and lack of emotion from the Sol Synths, that might not be possible.

6

Quintus

It took only an hour for Agatha to answer his call. He knew she would. The commander of the Base couldn't resist hearing what he had to say.

Quintus felt the usual tingle of a connection being made through his primary system. Arms folded, he waited for the Techs to enable the holographic imaging part of his programming.

The generic, white room changed. The dripping code and walls vanished slowly, and a plain office with a desk, two chairs and a filing cabinet overlaid it. Agatha's office in the Base, located inside the Bruno Mountain. A man-made cavern that housed the living quarters of the Sols and all relevant personnel—mostly Techs—involved in keeping the Sect safe. Segregated from the population behind high fences and brick walls. The place where Quintus had been trapped since his creation, doomed to spend the rest of his life watching the online traffic of the Sect residents, if Agatha had her way.

A shimmer began at his toes and raced up his legs to give him visibility in their world. Agatha, a dark-skinned woman aged around fifty years old, perched on the edge of her desk. She wore an electric-blue suit with a white blouse. Strong, bright colors were her preference. Her uniform was less formal than the Sols', with their black outfits, or the Techs', with their gray jackets with a double, vertical stripe down each breast pocket, and matching pants with a stripe down each leg.

The shimmer tapered off at his crown, then dissipated. From the sudden narrowing of her eyes he knew she could see him. In the glass window pane next to him, he caught a glimpse of his reflection. Today he was male, around forty years old, with a hooked nose and weak chin. What he looked like didn't matter—his image changed each time he presented in their world. What mattered was what he did—could do.

Quintus clasped his hands behind his back. 'Hello, Agatha. Long time no see.'

'Quintus.' She folded her arms. 'What's so urgent that you needed me to bring you out of the system?'

She said it with a slight sneer and that got his back up—or would have, if he had a back to get up. She was enjoying his incarceration too much.

'You mean *my* system. I built this damn place.'

'No, you *helped* to build this place. My Tech team programmed you with the ability to create.' She curled her upper lip. 'You didn't just appear out of thin air.'

Agatha still hadn't forgiven him. That much was obvious. He couldn't be sure she ever would. And all because of a little accident involving her father. He'd been lead Tech around here, pushing for greater diversified thinking among the sentient programs. It wasn't Quintus' fault that there had been a massive power surge at the *exact* moment Quintus had removed the safety limits on voltage. He'd only been doing what he'd been programmed to: think outside his parameters. It had been coincidence that someone had been working on the console. At that *exact* moment. And died.

'It wasn't my fault, you know.'

Agatha pressed her lips together. 'Is that what you want to talk about? Because we're done.'

She waved her hand—her move to terminate his hologram.

'Wait!' He held up his fading hand. 'That's not why I asked to see you.'

Agatha paused hers in mid air. 'Talk.'

Quintus released a low breath. 'Look, I know you don't want to give me anything more than my crappy permissions, but you have given me responsibility to spot security issues and report them. That's what I wanted to talk to you about... the latest software upgrade to the Synths.'

Agatha lowered her hand slowly. 'The Synths are no longer your concern.'

'No, but I helped design them, so who knows them better than me?'

'What you designed was a shell. What they are

now is due to the work my father did, and the Techs who still work here.'

True, he had been taken off the project early on. Agatha's father had also recommended that sentient programs not be in charge of sentient beings. What did they think he was going to do—start a revolution?

He pressed on. 'I noticed some code while I was sitting in my white room—a bit of color wouldn't go astray in there, you know—and I saw something that worried me.'

Agatha made a show of walking around to the other side of her desk and sitting down. She was nervous around him. That intrigued him, but it also made sure he would never escape his pallid room. If Quintus wanted to get out more, he had to prove he could be useful.

'What *about* the code?'

Despite the dead look in her eyes, her question gave him hope. It wasn't a dismissal.

Quintus took a step closer. She flinched, then wiped the look of fear from her expression and posture.

He continued. 'The upgrade last month, not the most recent one, also added behavioral modifications to the Synths. It gave them their hand twitch.'

'So?'

'Well, I noticed further modifications to the neural pathways were made, some that could conflict with their programming.'

He had no idea if there really was a conflict, but any risk might rattle Agatha. A rattled commander might let him help.

Agatha's eyes widened in apparent shock. 'Did you do something?'

Typical. One tiny accident and he would be labeled a miscreant forever.

'No I didn't *do* anything. What do you think I can actually get up to in my little room? I have access to mostly look, write some, never edit. Unless you want me to scrub your browsing history, I'd say that's the extent of my deviousness.'

Agatha crossed her arms again. Her favorite defensive position. 'I wouldn't put anything past you.'

'Trust me, you have me trapped inside a long tunnel of never-ending duties. I'm not going anywhere.'

'It's where you belong.'

He sighed. They were getting off topic. 'Look, I brought you this information because I thought it might help.'

Agatha's eyes narrowed. She stood and leaned on the table. A small smile danced across her lips. 'Ah, I see. This little chat isn't about doing the right thing. You want something in return. Your help for a favor.'

Why not?

'If this little snippet helps me broaden my horizons, then what's the harm?'

The commander of the Base stared at him. Then she laughed. 'Nice try, Quintus. I oversaw the change myself. The upgrade was a harmless one to fix physical bugs in the Synth's programming, and to smooth out personality temperament. The system reported no issues with any of the upgrades.'

Agatha lifted her hand a second time.

No... it's too soon.

He blurted out, 'No issues now, but what about in a week's time?'

She paused her hand again. 'What do you mean?'

'Look, I'm not here to mess you about, but I'm genuinely concerned with the behavior modifications I saw. They're incompatible with the ones that were initialized a month ago. You need to do more testing, make sure one isn't competing with the other. Or worse, one breaks a previous working update.'

'You think my Techs haven't thought of that?'

'Maybe they have, but I would be happy to take a look.'

This was what he craved—something juicy he could sink his proverbial teeth into.

Agatha smiled and shook her head. 'Nice try.'

She waved her hand and the scene became fat pixels before his eyes, turning back into his much despised, white room.

He cursed. Maybe he'd gone too far, been too cocky. Agatha was no pushover. But neither was he. He'd hoped the idea of incompatible updates might rattle the commander. Her father's death had happened because parameters had been broken. But she hadn't bought it.

Quintus paced his tiny room, which took six short steps to cross. The Synths were in no real danger as long as each upgrade was tested robustly. But he knew that the Techs often pulled double shifts at the Base before the upgrades were due. Mistakes were bound to be made. Who better to look after the sentients than another sentient? No need for sleep.

Quintus would keep pushing the commander, to see where Agatha's limits lay. To escape traffic duty he needed to be bold.

A soft voice boomed overhead. 'Hey, you okay in there?'

It was Shawn.

'Yeah, fine. Why?'

'Did you cry in front of Agatha, demand your own way again?'

'I don't—I did not—how dare—'

'Cool it. I'm only messing with you. You finish compiling the report on security issues like I asked?'

'Screw you!'

Shawn chuckled and clicked off.

Quintus stormed over to one wall, took a deep breath. He really had to stop letting the Techs get under his skin.

A new thought came to him. He turned from the wall and initialized comms from his end. 'Hey, Shawn?'

The line clicked open. 'Yeah?'

'I'm sorry for being a pain. I've had a bad day. I'll get right on it.'

'Yeah, you will.'

The line clicked off again. The Techs didn't trust him. He blamed Agatha for that.

The Sect

Quintus sat on his hard, plastic chair. It was clear that the commander had no interest in using him in any meaningful way ever again. Regardless of their positions, Shawn and Leo were just her yes men. The AI ran the mostly automated system, always had. A quick change to Quintus' permissions had put paid to that. He would be forced to play the dutiful sentient, doing what he could to help, within the parameters of what he was allowed to help with.

He stood. Four short steps from the chair to the only door and way out of read-write hell.

He reached for the handle just as energy built up and sparked. Quintus yanked his hand back and rubbed the pain out of it. The firewall designed to keep him in his construct was doing its job. But the Techs had to sleep some time. The automated session monitored his movements at night, but at least it didn't talk back or belittle him. Degrade him.

His chat with Agatha had left Quintus with no choice.

Within his limited capacity he would learn—about parameters, about loopholes, about boundaries. He'd explore again tonight, when the Techs clocked off for the night.

7

Cynthia

Mondays were the worst. The start of any new week grated on her, and the homework the teachers doled out seemed to never end. Cynthia walked to class, thinking about what she'd seen in the Mole zone. The breadth of their prejudice hadn't been entirely evident before now, but she had noticed an increase in the number of snide comments from the kids at school.

'Hey,' said Anya, sidling up to her.

Her shoulder-length, brown hair bobbed as she came to a fast stop.

'Hey.'

'How did the upgrade go?'

Cynthia shrugged. The upgrade had been so minor it could barely even be called that. 'Okay, I suppose.' She held out her hand. It was steady. 'The shake is gone.'

A couple of the girls in the corridor watched her. She dropped her hand to her side. Everyone knew what

Cynthia was here. She didn't hide her Synth status from anyone.

'That's good.' Anya looked around, noting the attention. She blushed. 'Uh, I guess we should get to History.'

'Sure, History. I'll be there in a minute. I just need to use the bathroom first.'

Cynthia watched Anya walk off to class. Something was off with her friend. She couldn't put her finger on it. Was it to do with their Mole encounter at Golden Gate Fields? Anya had flushed with embarrassment then, when the Mole had confronted Cynthia.

But the confrontation had come as a shock to Cynthia too. She hadn't done anything either.

Cynthia slipped into the bathroom and splashed cold water on her face. Her hand might not be shaking anymore, but a deeper shake lived in her body now, fueled by anger and fear. Two of the stall doors were closed. Cynthia could hear them moving about. She leaned on the wet, porcelain sink and stared at her reflection in the mirror. Words in red above the mirror caught her eye. She read the message scrawled in lipstick.

Synths out. That was it. Nothing else, except for a few messages around it, most in biro.

Yeah.

About time.

She swallowed down her anger.

The main door burst open and sharp laughter

reached her. A bloom of perfume assaulted her nose. Cynthia braced, recognizing one floral scent in particular.

'Girls,' said the lead girl with long, blonde hair, 'I cannot wait until the school realizes bathrooms are not for Synths. They are *not* real people.'

Cynthia looked over at Jessica, a Mole kid, and a nasty piece of work when she had a crowd. Dark blonde hair. Honey skin. Cute and vicious.

Her legion of fans tittered around her. The people in the stalls fell quiet.

Jessica's dulcet tones were swapped out for ones dripping with hate. 'What are you looking at, *Synth?*'

'Nothing interesting.'

'That's right, nothing interesting.'

'Hey,' piped up one of the girls. 'Is she saying you're not interesting, Jessica?'

Jessica's eyes seethed with hate. 'You'd better not be talking about me.'

Cynthia hadn't been, but she stifled a chuckle at the clever comeback.

The Mole kid eyed her. Cynthia knew better than to challenge this particular one.

Jessica strode up to her and punched her in the gut. Cynthia bent over with a groan.

'That's for whatever you're doing in here. Looking at your face in the mirror, huh? Well, there's nothing much to look at if you ask me.' Jessica turned for the door. 'Come on, girls. Let's get to class. See you in there, loser.'

The Sect

The mini tornado of girls exited, leaving just their cloud of perfume behind.

Two stalls flushed and a couple of girls Cynthia had seen around exited, both red faced.

'Uh, I'm sorry,' muttered one, as they washed their hands fast and left.

With a new breath, Cynthia composed herself and headed to class. Her stomach was not exactly like a human's but she felt pain there.

She took her usual seat in the second to last row, ignoring Jessica's eyes on her, and set her bag down by her feet. There was no sign of Anya.

She activated the screen attached to her desk and watched as the teacher at the top of the room organized papers on hers. Being the only Synth in this class hadn't bothered her before, but now it was all she could think about.

Her friend entered a few moments later, gaze everywhere but on Cynthia. Anya sat down in the seat next to Cynthia and fussed with her bag, as if she had something more important going on in there.

Mumbling began two rows ahead of her. Two of the girls from Jessica's legion glanced back at Cynthia.

She couldn't make out what they were saying, but then one of the girls muttered 'half breed' over her shoulder. The others in the class giggled, until the teacher shouted for everyone to be quiet.

Cynthia balled her fists under her table. More Mole propaganda. More lies that one well-behaving Synth could do nothing about.

The offensive girl was another from the Mole zone. The class had three, maybe four Mole children in the class. But those who were laughing now weren't just Moles. Some were Tech and Neer children. Some were Earthers.

Cynthia glanced at Anya. She had her head down, nose in her book, pretending like she couldn't hear. But the blush on her cheeks said she'd heard.

It was hard not to. The whole damn class had heard it.

'Idiots,' Cynthia growled at her friend.

But Anya only responded with a closed smile.

'Go back to your master,' the same Mole girl whispered back at Cynthia.

More laughter ensued.

'Go scrap yourself,' Jessica said.

More reprimands from the teacher followed. Not that the adults ever did a damn thing to truly curb the bullying.

The teacher began the lesson and both Jessica and the Mole girl turned to face the front.

'Okay, could everyone please turn to section eight on their screens?' said the teacher. 'Today we'll be studying the creation of the Sects in United America and their alignment with policies in the European Nations.'

Cynthia flicked to the section and sighed.

The teacher continued. 'Ten years ago, before the war with the Australasia and Japan Colonies, New San Francisco was forced to adopt the Corp's "Sect" model, designed to protect the coast from foreign invasion. Becoming a Sect meant erecting a high wall around its perimeter, and exiling those who didn't fit the prerequisite skills. New San Francisco wasn't the only city in United America to become a Sect. Others along its coast did too. But with the war over, the Sect model remained in place. Today, trade occurs only between the Sects, and they benefit from additional funding from the European Nations. After the war United America split in two, creating colonies, which contain both Sects and regular cities. The Corp is working on setting up more colonies, hoping to convince the remaining cities that they would be better off under the new design. That they, too, can reap the rewards of shared power.'

Cynthia tuned out of the lesson. She knew all this. It was in one of her files, there since her inception. More colonies was a recent thing. The Corp was pushing it.

Jessica turned around and mouthed, *Go scrap yourself and die.*

Her only friend still said nothing, just bit her lip. But Cynthia noticed her hands were two fists. At least it was a reaction. Not a great one, but hey.

She could handle a few ignorant girls. But her best friend believing the lies?

That she could not bear.

8

Anya

'That boy is going to eat me out of house and home!'

With a sigh, Grace slammed the fridge door closed.

Anya sat at the kitchen table shelling the beans for dinner. The edge of her mouth lifted. Anything that shone a bad spotlight on Jason was a good thing in her books. She still felt sick over what had happened during history class, and how she'd allowed Jessica and that Mole girl to make rude comments to Cynthia.

Her father wandered into the room, his reading glasses perched on the end of his nose. 'Trouble?'

Grace turned sharply and waved at the fridge. 'Nothing, Evan. Except your eighteen-year-old son is putting away food like he's eating for three.'

Anya suppressed a giggle with her fist.

Evan removed his glasses. 'He's a growing boy, love. He needs sustenance.'

'Well, I'd prefer it if he'd let me know the next

time he plans to clean me out of food. I'm out of butter, eggs *and* milk.'

An exasperated Grace turned away. Her gaze flitted around for a moment, then settled on Anya.

Anya tensed up. 'No, no... No!'

Why her? Why not the garbage disposal unit posing as her brother?

Grace extended her hand out to Anya's and pressed the backs of their hands together. Anya's chip pinged with new credit.

She smiled sweetly. 'Don't be long, honey.'

Anya stood up roughly. 'I wasn't the one who ate all the food in this house! Why do I have to go get more?'

'Because you're a good girl,' said Evan. 'And good girls do as their mothers say.'

'Not all of them,' Anya muttered.

Grace's voice lifted. 'What did you say?'

'Nothing.' She pinched the bridge of her nose. 'Mother, this is a teachable moment. If you send Jason to get the food, he'll be less likely to eat it all in the future. You're making it too easy for him.'

Grace waved her hand at her. 'That boy is so busy these days studying for his Neer exams. Besides, he won't remember to get the brown eggs, not the white ones. You're much better at it. Mama's little helper.'

'You mean her little slave?'

Grace steered Anya out of the kitchen with a small shove. 'Get going, now. I need you back as soon as possible. You still need to peel the potatoes. And don't dawdle at the market.'

'Like I ever have time to do that.'

She made sure to huff loud enough to be heard before storming out of the room. Jason, the saint. The growing boy. The untouchable. *Don't worry, Jason, the women will clean up after you.*

'Argh!'

It was so sexist she wanted to scream.

Ω

The journey from train to Zone One and the largest Earthers' market took longer on foot in her haze of anger. A suitable punishment for Jason accompanied each step to the warehouse in the vicinity of Pier 45.

She entered the enclave, a basic, brick warehouse filled with a collection of stalls around the edge, and three rows in the middle. The clean smell of freshly caught fish reached her—a consignment from one of the other Sects. A healthy fish supply used to thrive once in the Bay's mix of saltwater and freshwater. All that existed now were the tiny plankton the fish used to feed on. The Sect relied on trade from similar cities and Earthers, to keep the residents fed.

People from Zones Two to Six gathered, some browsing, some paying for goods with a wave of their hand. Transactional beeps underpinned the hum of conversation.

Anya walked with her head held high and headed straight for the stall with dairy. The sooner she got started the sooner she could leave.

She lifted her hand and checked her mother's shopping list. Anya groaned. It was much longer than the few things she'd claimed Jason had eaten.

With a roll of her eyes, she shuffled over to the dairy stall. Two people were ahead of her. The person in front of her, an older man around fifty, smelled of grease and oil. His hands, black with dirt, weren't much cleaner than his overalls. A Mole.

Anya's breath quickened. She'd been no friend to Cynthia that day in Golden Gate Fields, nor had she stood up for her when the kids in school had given her a hard time. It seemed the Moles were always finding something else to complain about. Worse, the Neer kids were now picking up their bad habits. Anya didn't know how to stop it. She was only one person.

Ahead of the Mole was a woman. She looked around; Anya noticed warmth in her eyes. Her hands were slender, clean. Anya guessed she was either a Tech or a Neer. She didn't have the engineered physicality to be a Sol, nor did she have their cool temperament. The Sols had a more authoritative air about them. The Techs and Neers rarely got their hands dirty—literally. The Earthers and Moles regularly worked with their hands. She checked her own. A little black dirt was lodged under the nails from preparing dinner. She picked them clean.

The Mole ahead of her mumbled something inaudible under his breath. Without warning, he shoved the woman ahead of him, knocking her to the ground.

Anya stumbled back in shock.

The man squared up to the Earther behind the counter. 'It's not right you're servin' one of them before me.'

'One of what?'

'A Synth!'

The stall owner frowned at him. 'She's not a Synth. I'd be able to tell.'

'She is.' The man pointed at the fallen woman. 'I saw her left hand shake just now.'

Cynthia's hand used to shake, but since her upgrade, the shake had vanished. Anya was certain the man had not seen anything of the sort. It was most likely he just had an issue with waiting in line.

'Look, she was here first,' said the stall owner.

The woman looked up at the man, from her position on the ground. Her gaze flickered to Anya, then back to the man. Anya saw fear lodged in her eyes. And that's when she understood. She was a Synth, all right.

Anya imagined Cynthia lying in her place and her anger flared. She went to the woman and helped her to her feet.

'Whatcha doin' there, girlie?' The Mole rounded on her. 'Why you helpin' one of them?'

'What, a Neer?' Anya said with as much confidence as she could fake.

The man scoffed. 'She's no Neer.' He pointed. 'I saw her hand shake.'

'No you didn't, because she's not a Synth. Her

kid goes to my school.'

The Mole froze and cursed. It was well known that Synths could not reproduce.

With a cough, he recovered from his shock. To the woman he said, 'Yeah, well, next time hurry the hell up. I got things to do. I'm on the clock.'

The Moles had the longest work schedule of all the skills. The Earthers came a close second in terms of hours logged. Anya wondered if the Synths represented a privileged life the Moles could never attain. Perhaps jealousy was their main motive for intimidation, not fear.

Commotion started at one end of the warehouse. Three Sols burst into the space, their thick boots slamming in perfect time against the concrete floor of the market.

'Crap, they must have been close by,' muttered the Earther stall owner.

One Sol stormed up to the counter. He was young, around eighteen, with a thick neck and broad shoulders. His overdeveloped physique didn't match his young face.

'Is there a problem here?' he barked at the Earther.

The Mole sneered and pointed a finger at the woman. 'Yeah, this Synth tried to cut in line.'

'No, I didn't—I—'

The Sol turned to Anya, as if she were the only witness. 'Is that what happened?'

She held her breath, flicked her gaze to the

woman again; her lips were drawn thin and white. Then she looked at the Mole, who stared at her with a curled lip and blackened eyes.

'No. This Mole's a liar,' she breathed out. Her heart slammed against her ribs. 'And she's a Neer. I told him her kid goes to my school.'

The Sol eyed the woman for a moment, then turned to the Mole and twisted his arm behind his back. Anya heard a crack. The Mole let out a sickening scream.

'My arm! You broke it!'

'That will teach you to lie,' said the Sol as coldly as the move was calculated.

The Mole folded over. 'I can't work with a broken arm. You gonna compensate me for lost earnings?'

'Shut your mouth, Mole, and be glad I didn't break your legs too.'

The Sol shoved the Mole hard in the chest. He stumbled back, righted himself and grabbed a carton of eggs.

'Payment,' he muttered.

The Sol's mouth pinched, but he didn't pursue him. He simply turned and rejoined his crew. Then the three Sols left.

The woman held out her shaking hand to the Earther. 'For the eggs he stole. Put it on my tab.'

The Earther scanned it. 'You didn't have to do that.'

'I know.' She turned to Anya slowly. 'I'm not a

Neer.'

Anya smiled sadly. 'I know. Be careful.'

With a brief nod and weak smile, the woman left.

Anya steadied her breaths, which were coming out shallow and painful now. Her hands shook as the adrenaline left her system.

The Earther watched her. 'You ready to order, miss?'

She called out from Grace's list, collected her things and paid for it all with a swipe of her hand. Then she continued around the market, collecting the rest of the list. Her jitters made carrying the goods more difficult, but at least she'd been able to help the Synth. In some small way, she had eased the guilt over not protecting her friend.

$$\Omega$$

Dinnertime was a chatty affair. Jason and a few of his budding Neer classmates had formed a study group. He would be practicing with them in the evening time. A distracted Anya did little more than shove her food around the plate. The easing of guilt had not lasted long. Her thoughts had soon drifted back to Cynthia.

Grace frowned at her. 'You've been awfully quiet since you came home with the shopping. Is everything okay?'

Anya flicked her gaze at her then away. 'Fine.'

Evan poked her shoulder gently. 'Are you still angry with your mother about having to do the shopping? Because we all have to help out around here.'

'No, I just have stuff on my mind.'

'Like what?' Evan probed.

She had no interest in talking about it. Jason could barely contain his disdain for Synths. Her parents would probably scold her for helping one today.

Anya shoved her chair back. 'May I be excused?'

Grace waved her hand at Anya. 'If you must, moody girl. Off you go.'

Anya took the stairs two at a time and entered the bedroom that was all hers. At least she and Jason were too old to share anymore. The interior walls of the two-bedroomed house had been reworked to accommodate three smaller spaces.

She threw herself on the bed. Flipping onto her back, she held up her hand and called Cynthia. Her friend answered after three rings.

'Hey, what's up, Mighty Mortal?' Cynthia said.

Anya smiled. Her friend could always put her in a better mood. It relieved her to see she'd forgotten about the drama in class.

'I don't suppose you heard about what happened down at the market today?'

Cynthia nodded and tapped the side of her head. 'Not many secrets among the Synths. Thanks for helping Angela.'

'I wish I didn't have to.' She hated how segregated the skills were becoming. 'The Sol broke that man's arm, like it was a twig.'

The Sect

'They're strong. And getting stronger with the new batch of muscle-enhancing injections.'

Anya transferred the call to the monitor on the desk next to her bed, giving her back control of both hands. She used them to hug her body. 'I had things under control. Then the Sol butted in and made things worse. Mistrust is creeping into the zones, but the Corp doesn't care about how its military is controlling the Sect.'

'It's been that way for a long time, Anya.' Her friend shrugged. 'I don't see things changing soon.'

She didn't believe Cynthia would prefer that things stayed the same. 'I wish the Corp would do more to fix the problems in the Sect. We aren't Exiles. We deserve respect.'

Last month, the Corp had projected their leader's image onto a fifty-feet-high hologram, to report stats. A woman with a kind face, gentle smile and easy posture. Crime rates were down, she said. Harmony and wellbeing had increased by three percent this month compared to last month.

Like that was true. If the Corp actually dared to show up in the flesh instead of living in their fancy, fenced-off real estate far from the Sect and the Exiles, maybe they would see the actual problems this colony design of theirs had.

Cynthia was watching her closely. Too closely. It unnerved her.

Something was off with her friend. Anya didn't want to consider the upgrade might have anything to do with that change. She tried not to think about how, with each upgrade, Cynthia inched closer to the end of her first life cycle. They were fighting more than usual. The treatments seemed to be jamming a wedge between them.

With a deep breath, Anya brushed aside her negativity. 'How are you feeling?'

Cynthia's eyes widened slightly. 'Feeling? I'm fine.'

This was the perfect time to apologize for her behavior in school today. But Anya hesitated. 'Er, still no issues with the upgrade?'

Cynthia held out her hand. It was rock steady. 'The twitch is gone. I'm glad.' She lowered her hand. 'Other than that, all good.'

Anya attempted a smile. 'I'm glad.'

But her friend didn't return the smile. She knew her moods too well.

'I gotta go.' Cynthia paused. 'Don't worry, Anya. This Sect will figure things out. You'll see.'

9

Quintus

'Aargh!'

Quintus banged his fist on the white wall. The constant *drip drip drip* of code rippled.

He'd spent the last few days hunting for a loophole that would give him a way out of his prison. He'd found nothing. The damn Techs had been exemplary in their nightly lock-up routine, which was unsurprising, since Agatha ran a tight ship. But Quintus had come to expect less of humans. Techs were the super smart exception to the human rule—they'd kept him locked up for this long, and that was no mean feat—but all humans had flaws.

He paced his tiny room with its questionable décor and lone exit. He walked over to the door and the room with edit access, and tried the handle again. The firewall delivered him a hefty shock, forcing him backward.

He shook the pain out of his hand.

'Think, Quintus, think.'

Even his name wasn't his. His creator had had an interest in old languages. Quintus, meaning five, denoted he was the fifth in a series of creations. Four lesser creations had come before him, but his creator, seeking perfection, had stopped at five. He looked around his prison and laughed bitterly. Maybe the earlier four had been the lucky ones.

Quintus strode over to the code that rarely changed unless there was an update. Newer code showed up as red for a short time, before it faded to the usual off-white. He'd stared at the string of numbers and letters for close to a week now. No upgrades had shown up that he could manipulate by reporting false anomalies, no downtime was scheduled during which he might learn how to get around their latest firewall rules.

He folded himself on the floor with a heavy sigh.

A familiar voice boomed over the communication channel. 'What's all the ruckus in there?'

It was Shawn, the Tech with a short attention span on occasion. Quintus was still waiting for him to forget something, to mess up. But whenever Quintus wanted something to happen was exactly the time it didn't. This past week, Shawn's routines and attention to detail had been faultless.

'Nothing. I'm just bored,' he replied with a sigh, hoping to distract Shawn with some idle chatter.

'You got nothing to do in your little, white room? What about the traffic? Your last report said there was a spike in usage on Saturday. Anything further to add?'

'Usual weekend activity.'

The kids tended to sit around talking to each other. It always accounted for half of the spike.

'What about security analysis?'

'Finished my checks last night.'

'So get started on today's report.'

It wasn't due for a few hours. The script he'd written had automated the process. Shawn and Leo had no idea that what used to take Quintus hours was now a ten-minute job.

'Good idea...' Quintus trailed off as something Shawn said caught his attention. 'How do you know this room is white?' He got to his feet, his gaze searching the space. 'You watching me in here?'

Shawn laughed. 'I've got better things to do than babysit you. Nah, I saw the construct before they stuck you in there. I understand how big—or small, I should say—it is, and that you've got a door at one end.'

Quintus' curiosity was piqued. Shawn was being surprisingly chatty today. 'If you know all that, then you also know I can barely breathe in here. I'm going crazy in this tight space. I need out once in a while. Or at least assign me a bigger room.'

'No can do. Agatha's orders. The space you have is all the space you're gonna get. She doesn't like you.'

Tell me something I don't know.

Quintus was about to say more when a second voice joined the conversation.

'Who you talking to?'

It was Leo, the Tech more senior than Shawn.

'Quintus, who else? He's throwing a tantrum in there for some reason.'

He wasn't throwing a tantrum. He wasn't a baby. He resented the accusation.

'Well, forget about that,' said Leo. 'It's Darryl's birthday and there's cake in the kitchen. You want me to bring you some?'

'Nah, I'll come with. I don't need to watch Quintus. He's not going anywhere.'

Quintus heard a click and the voices vanished. Birthday cake? It wasn't the first time the staff had been lured away with promises of cake. What was the appeal there? He'd never eaten food. He had no physical body except for when he manifested as a hologram. But that was all smoke and mirrors. He couldn't interact with anything in holographic mode.

With a heavy sigh, Quintus slumped against the wall. The code diverted from the wall to flow over him. Something flashed in a section of it. A yellow piece of code. He pushed off from the wall and turned to examine it. The lock on his prison hadn't been properly secured.

His neurons fired nervously as he considered the possibility Shawn had slipped up. He walked over to the door, then hesitated. He reached out for the handle but nothing sparked, nothing drove him a hard foot back.

Quintus chuckled. 'Thank you, birthday cake.'

He opened the door and peered inside the next

room. This one was dark gray in appearance with lighter gray code running down the walls. He stepped inside the room. No alarms sounded. But Shawn wouldn't be gone for long, and would soon discover his mistake. He had to work fast.

Quintus strode up to the code on one wall and memorized the repeating pattern. The Synths' operational code.

He cursed.

It was all here. How many were in operation, what operational system they were running on, when they were due their next upgrade, and what security patches had been applied. The information on the second-life-cycle Synths was locked out—a necessary security measure since some of them worked as Sols for Agatha. But the information on the first-life-cycle Synths was wide open.

Quintus ran through the potential of his find. What could he do here? Insert a piece of broken code, make the Synths go off the rails? What good would that do him stuck inside the Base? Nothing.

No, he needed more than that. He studied the code some more.

'What's your end goal, Quintus?' he muttered. 'To get out of here.'

He replied to himself. 'So, do that.'

But how could he? He had no form in the real world, no way of activating control panels. What he needed was someone to break him out of read-write hell and get him into the primary systems. But to do that, it would have to be someone special. The Techs didn't care enough to free him, and Agatha would be happy if he never got out. But the Synths... he'd created them. Could he use them in some way?

He memorized the software code for the next upgrade. Maybe he could slip something extra in there, some primary command that would lure them here so they could get him out. The Synths might look and act human, but underneath the skin and blood they were still machines.

Quintus had one finger almost on the code, ready to deliver something extra, when he heard a fast, clicking noise.

'No...' he breathed out.

Shawn was logging into the system. Soon, he'd discover that he'd left the door unlocked and find Quintus missing. He raced for the door and slipped past it, returning to the dazzling, white room that would have given him a headache—if he had a head to get one in. With a soft click the door closed—and just in time. A surge of power bloomed at his fingertips. He snatched his hand away and backed up, neurons firing at double speed through his system.

Shawn's voice shook. 'Uh, Quintus, you there?'

He slid to the floor, body stiff. 'Present.'

He heard Shawn breathe out a sigh of relief.

Quintus worked to lighten the tension he felt. 'Uh, how was the birthday cake?'

'Ah, I've had better. If it's not chocolate, it's not cake.'

Shawn clicked off and left Quintus to formulate his new plan. But getting inside the edit room a second time would take patience, skill and a whole lot of luck.

He walked over to his console and studied the code he could manipulate. It was back-end stuff that controlled the lights, allowed him to change the appearance of his room from white to off-white. Nothing useful.

But could he use his limited control to insert partial bits of code into the running of this place, force a physical change inside the Base?

An idea came to him. He quickly isolated strings of data. It didn't take long before he found what he was looking for.

Why he hadn't thought of this before?

The old security patches that were no longer valid had been dumped in his trash. He could see them, but he couldn't enable them. What he *could* do was rename the files. He knew the naming convention the Techs used for the patches. If he renamed an older patch to look like a newer update, the system might enable it. All he had to do was slip the renamed file into the correct folder and wait.

He tried it, pulling an older patch out of the bin and giving it a new name. Then he moved it into place so the system could see it. Enabling an older patch wouldn't remove the current one, but it might disrupt things in the real world.

With the patch in place he waited.

The changes to the code started out small, quickly

branching out in new directions, like a virus spreading inside the programming. An alarm sounded somewhere. The comms link clicked on. Quintus heard two voices, one Shawn's, the other Leo's. Except the conversation wasn't directed at him.

'What the hell's going on?' said Leo. 'What did you do?'

'Nothing!' replied Shawn. 'The security patch, it's doing weird stuff.'

'Lemme see.'

Shuffling followed and lots of tapping.

'Crap, something is tying the system up in knots,' said Leo. 'But I don't understand. The current security patch is still active. It's still working.' He sighed. 'I'm gonna need a minute to figure this out.'

'Do you want me to tell Agatha?' asked Shawn.

'Not yet. Let's see if I can fix it first.'

Quintus checked the code that was slowly changing on his wall. Features in the older patch were conflicting with the newer one. The lights in his tiny prison dimmed, then brightened. That meant there was a dip in power being delivered to his room.

Apparently, disrupting the lights in the Base sent the team into a panic. Good to know.

10

Anya

'What did you score on your English test today?'

Anya was lying on her bed, her hand raised high above her head, as she chatted with her best friend.

Cynthia shrugged. 'Eighty-five percent. You?'

'Sixty.'

A pass wasn't bad for a subject she could barely tolerate.

'You'll do better next time.'

Cynthia seemed quieter than usual. Or maybe she was just picking up on Anya's hesitant mood. They still hadn't talked about what happened in history class, three days ago. Anya knew she was only making it worse by keeping quiet on the matter. But she had no idea how to bring it up. She had allowed her friend to take Jessica's abuse. She should have defended her.

'Look, what happened—'

The lights went out in Anya's bedroom, plunging it into instant darkness. Her comms device cut out in the middle of her conversation with Cynthia.

'What the hell...?'

She tried to reconnect to Cynthia, but the connectivity wheel—faded but just about visible—circled in the space before her. Anya scrambled off the bed and felt her way to the door. She heard voices and footsteps coming up the stairs.

'Kids?'

It was Evan. Anya opened the door, but without windows on the landing she couldn't see a thing. She heard a second door click open.

'What's going on?' Jason said.

She barely made out his outline.

'A power outage,' Evan said. 'I just got a call on the dial-up communicator. We need to leave the house now.'

Jason sighed heavily next to her ear, which meant he was too close for her liking.

'Damn Techs,' he muttered. 'Think they know everything and break stuff they don't understand. That's why I'm becoming a Neer. They learn about the architecture of how something works. Figure that out and you can build things to last.'

The damn Techs this, the saintly Neers that. Any opportunity for Jason to complain about the Techs, he took it. It seemed like that's all he was doing lately. He barely acknowledged Cynthia whenever she dropped round for a visit.

'Come on,' Grace said, as loud as Evan had been. Anya hadn't heard her come up the stairs. She was but a voice. 'Leave your stuff and grab your coats.'

Anya hesitated. Grace was asking a lot from a teenager to abandon her things. She relied on tech to keep in touch with the world.

'I just want to get a few things...'

She gripped the door frame and peered into her bedroom. She could pack her school bag fast. It wouldn't take a moment to feel around for the things that mattered.

'No time, Anya,' said Evan. He sounded nearer now. 'Come on.'

A hand on her arm—Evan's, she presumed—pulled her out and guided her to the railing. She grabbed it and slid along it to take herself to the top of the stairs, then down.

An impatient Jason followed. 'Hurry up.'

No way was she breaking her neck for him.

A small trickle of light fed through the window of the front door, giving partial illumination to the living room. She froze on one step when she caught a glimpse of black fabric and hardened body armor outside.

Jason bumped into her and cursed. 'Why have you stopped?'

Sols were outside their house, and they had flashlights. One of the men tapped on the door with what she presumed was the base of one.

'Out now,' the Sol ordered.

She heard similar commands echo outside. They must be going door to door.

Evan made it to the ground floor fast and opened

the front door.

'We're coming,' he said to the waiting Sol. 'We've got two kids here, so please don't alarm them. Do you know what happened?'

'Power outage at the Base,' the Sol said. 'Precautionary. You need to hurry. The facilities we're taking you to will provide you with everything you need.'

'Are you sure we can't stay here?' Grace pushed. 'Seems like overkill to ship us off to a facility for one little outage.'

The Sol shook his head. 'No exceptions. I don't make the rules.'

Evan ushered Anya out the door. She just had time to grab her coat. An unseasonal autumn chill in the air nipped at her skin, forcing her to slip her coat on. Grace followed with Jason. Together, they shuffled along their alley to the main street, where a bus was waiting. They climbed on board and took their seats alongside other residents. The bus moved off.

Each Sect had a Base. The problem was everything within the Sect operated from that Base. It controlled everything—light, heat, power. Yeah, they could stay at the house, if the outage only lasted a short while. But the longer the problem persisted, the longer it would take for life to return to normal. Anya loved tech, but sometimes it was hard to move two inches without it controlling some aspect of her life.

The bus trundled along a long street next to the wall of their zone, between Five and Four. The trains whizzed overhead. Anya saw they were crammed with people. The bus arrived at the gate that would lead to Four. Someone opened it and the bus drove through. They passed through similar gates, reaching the last one and Zone One. Then it took the street leading to Pier 45.

Were they going to Alcatraz? She didn't remember an outage happening before so she had nothing to compare it to.

She turned to her father. 'How long do these outages usually last?'

Evan shook his head. 'First time for me. The Base has never suffered a power failure before.'

She sat back in her seat, and watched the darkened streets and buildings whip by the window. What had happened at the Base? Anya knew so little about the military stronghold that was located inside the San Bruno Mountain, except that it had been built by the Corp to control the Sect. Cynthia's updates also came from there, delivered to the Station and the upload pods it housed.

She shivered as the late evening air turned chillier. The bus joined a line of other buses leading to a warehouse-type facility by the water's edge. From inside the bus she caught the familiar smell of salt in the air from the Bay's estuary. Bright floodlights lit up the warehouse, which was surrounded by a chain-link fence. More Sols than usual swarmed the area. She'd seen this place from the viewing platform in Golden Gate Fields. Trainee Sols would gather here before boarding the train to the island.

Ten minutes later, a Sol instructed her and others to get off.

Anya waited for her parents to make the first move. Jason lounged in the seat next to hers, like it would take a crane to remove him. The first of the passengers filed off the bus. But then a noise came through the Sol's ear piece; he stopped the next passenger from getting off.

'Wait—' he barked.

The Sol appeared to be listening to someone. Was it the Base? Or was it someone from the Corp, the faceless corporation that stamped its logo everywhere, and that continued to push the US region outliers, like the Dakotas and Colorado, into becoming Sects?

'How long?' the Sol asked the mystery person on the other end of the line. Then he nodded and fanned his hands at the passengers. 'Everyone back in their seats. Power has been restored.'

Anya looked behind her to see the city's lights turn on in a wavelike pattern. She saw Jason still hadn't moved. She sat down beside him.

He grunted. 'All for nothing as usual. The Techs are useless.'

If only Anya had thought to grab her earplugs, then she could drown out his incessant whining.

Evan and Grace returned to their seat in front of them.

Her father turned and smiled. 'See, nothing to worry about. The Sect is well organized. The people at the Base know what they're doing.'

'Yeah,' Anya managed to say.

She held out her hand and gave a soft sigh. Her comms device was coming back online. A world without tech terrified her. Why would she ever want to live rough like the Exiles?

The bus turned around and headed for the gates between the zones. Before leaving Zone One, she looked back at the San Bruno Mountain, where the Base was located. Only Techs and Sols were allowed in there.

The bus drove through the gate, and the mountain vanished behind rows of houses. Anya settled in her seat.

Maybe she should give both skills serious consideration. Being out of the loop sucked.

11

Cynthia

Anya's face vanished off her screen without warning. Cynthia's bedroom plunged into darkness at the same time. She snapped her hand closed and looked around the black space. She waited a moment for her Synth eyes with their extra abilities to adjust to the new space. Her night vision turned the darkness into greens and grays. It assisted her as she scrambled off her bed and left the room in search of her parents. Both human, they had no such optical advantage.

She called out to them. She heard an 'Ow!' followed by some shuffling downstairs. Cynthia took the stairs two at a time, finding her parents in the living room in a state of confusion.

She gripped an arm of each of her parents. 'It's okay, I'm here.'

'Oh Cynthia, there you are,' her mother breathed out.

Cynthia guided their hands to the back of the

sofa, and when they both had a grip, she released her hold. 'I'll get some torches.'

'Check in the cupboard below the stairs,' said her father.

She had taken two steps away from them when a sharp pounding, like a fist being used, permeated through the door. 'Open up now!'

She peered out through the glass in the front door. Her night vision showed her the perfect outline of a thick-necked Sol in the standard, black uniform.

'Who is it?' asked her mother.

'A Sol,' she replied.

More pounding followed. 'Open up now, or we'll break the door down.'

Cynthia lunged for the handle and opened it.

'That's not necessary—' she squeaked.

Four soldiers piled into the house, forcing Cynthia back.

One rounded on her. 'Are you the only Synth in this house at this present time?'

Her heart pounded at the mention of what she was.

'Yeah,' she squeaked again, her voice an octave higher than usual.

Living with human parents was supposed to integrate her into society, not separate her further from it.

One of the Sols grabbed her arm roughly. She jerked away from his grip, but he was too strong. The Sols always were.

Panicked, Cynthia glanced over her shoulder to see both her parents squinting into the dark.

'Where are you taking her?' said her mother.

'Stay put, ma'am,' said the Sol holding Cynthia. 'This doesn't concern you.'

Her mother straightened up, anger flashing across her face. 'Of course it concerns me. She's my daughter.'

In that moment Cynthia couldn't have loved her adopted mother more, ready to defend her, even though she wasn't her flesh and blood.

'It's okay,' she said to them. 'It's just routine.'

'Routine what?' her father demanded, taking a step forward.

But the darkness limited his step to just one.

'Stay put,' demanded the Sol. 'Someone will be along for you shortly.'

The discussion ended the second the Sol pulled her out the front door and into the alley. With the other Sols having returned to the main street, her Sol dragged Cynthia to them. A bus waited.

'Get on board,' he ordered her.

She did, realizing fast she wasn't alone. Other teenagers sat on the bus. She recognized a few from school—all Synths, all first life cycle. If she were to hazard a guess, so were the rest on the bus.

Cynthia sat down on one seat and shifted across to the window. She looked out at the chaos as more Sols dragged surprised-looking girls and boys out of their houses. It didn't take long before the bus was full.

Without any explanation given, the bus started to move.

'Where are we going?' whispered one girl to another in the seat in front of Cynthia.

They were young, maybe thirteen years old.

'I don't know,' came the shaky reply.

Cynthia tried to swallow down the lump of fear lodged in her throat. All around, the streets were as dark as her room had been. Did they suspect the Synths had something to do with the power outage, was that it?

The bus took a familiar route into Zone One, and when it turned onto the main street, she knew where they were headed.

The Station, the place where she received her monthly upgrade. The bus pulled up outside the dark, glass building and a Sol ordered them off. She did what she was told, still not sure why they'd been brought there. Cynthia shivered in the cold evening air. She hadn't been given time to grab her jacket.

Heavily armed Sols lined the way inside the building. Cynthia hugged herself, a little for warmth, but mostly for protection. She'd never seen so many Sols gathered in one area before.

Inside wasn't much better. A thick line of Sols guarded the entrance and both walls inside the Station, which still had power. In the middle was a group of frightened, young Synths.

'Where are the second-life-cycle Synths?' She asked one of the Sols.

If they were rounding up all synthetics, then they should be here too. The Sol grunted and shoved her toward the group of Synths.

Cynthia waited next to them. At least the Station was marginally warmer than the outside. But why was she here? What were they worried about specifically? Why had the Sol told her parents to wait, that someone was coming for them?

Nervous whispers filled the space. The Sols didn't reprimand anyone. They just stared blankly ahead of them, like the unfeeling soldiers they were trained to be.

'Maybe we're getting an upgrade,' one of the girls whispered behind her.

Maybe that was it. Or perhaps, during a power outage, the safest thing to do was to protect the Synths from a possible wireless hack. There could be a hundred reasons for the power going out, but one was always that it had been targeted deliberately. First-life-cycle Synths were more vulnerable to power outages. Their systems could be hacked more easily because of the security vulnerability of software upgrades. Less of the second-life-cycle Synths' code was accessible, and what little was online had nothing to do with command functionality that could be interfered with.

Cynthia stood taller, feeling better for figuring out the reason for this gathering.

One of the Sols spoke into his wrist, then whispered something to an older man, whom Cynthia assumed was in charge.

'Stand down,' the older man shouted to the Sols. 'This training exercise is over. Please return the Synths to their homes.'

As fast as they had arrived they were loaded onto the buses again. The city popped back into life. Streets lights cast a pale-orange glow over the gray-colored roads. Previously lit rooms flipped from darkness to a pale yellow.

'Well, that was weird,' one boy said to another when they were back on the bus.

They both laughed, a nervous titter.

Cynthia took her old seat and gripped the one in front of her. A training exercise? Her most recent upgrade had not included any information about that.

The crisis was over, for now. But a training exercise for what?

The bus destined for Zone Five sped through the gates and let her off where it had picked her up. She followed the alley way back to her front door. Inside, she found the lights on and both of her parents pacing.

Her mother rushed to her and pulled her into a hug. Cynthia snuggled into her warmth.

'Oh, thank God. Nobody was telling us anything. We feared the worst had happened.'

Cynthia pulled back. 'Worst?'

Her mother hesitated.

But her father nodded. 'Tell her.'

'We heard rumors that the first-life-cycle Synths can be terminated if an outage lasts too long. Something to do with them being vulnerable to attack.' Her mother stroked her hair. 'But everything's fine.'

Terminated? Since when was that a thing? She'd

been preparing to move from first life cycle to second. None of that included a threat to her existence.

She pulled out of her mother's reach and smiled weakly. 'Excuse me, I'm tired. I think I'll turn in early.'

'Of course.' Her mother smiled. 'We're happy you're okay.'

Cynthia took the stairs two at a time and called Anya. Her best friend's worried face popped up.

'Cyn, thank God you're okay. I was worried.'

She looked too relieved. Had Anya also heard the rumors?

Cynthia sat down on the bed. 'What happened tonight? Did Sols come for you?'

Anya nodded, her eyes wide. 'We were taken to the warehouse close to Pier 45. Dad said it was safer since the houses rely on so much power. What happened to you?'

'I was separated from my parents and taken to the Station. All the first-cycle Synths were.'

Anya frowned. 'Why?'

She studied her friend's confused reaction. Maybe she hadn't heard the rumors. She felt better.

'They said it was a training exercise. But my mother told me something else tonight. She said the first-life-cycle Synths risk being terminated during a power outage.'

Anya pulled back, her mouth as wide as her eyes. 'What? Since when?'

Cynthia didn't remember there ever being a power outage before. The Base had steady control over the Sect. 'Dunno, but it shocked the hell out of me. I was terrified.'

Her heart still hadn't returned to a regular rhythm.

Anya's face drew nearer. 'Why would they even do that? What's the point?'

'I guess it's a risk if someone uses the outage to hack one of us, turn us against the humans?' She shrugged, feeling sick about it. 'When the system comes back online, maybe one of us or all gets something additional in our programming.'

'That's barbaric! Surely they can't think that's a solution to anything. I mean, they created you, they upgrade your software monthly to avoid this exact thing.'

'I didn't think it was a solution at all.'

Her heart grew heavy as she remembered the propaganda she'd seen in Zone Six, and Anya's bland reaction when the girls in school had said nasty things to Cynthia.

'Look, I just called to check in on you quickly,' Cynthia added. 'I'm exhausted and I need to go to bed.'

Anya pulled back. 'Sure, of course. And Cynth?'

'Yeah?'

'I won't let anything bad happen to you. I'm sorry for not defending you in Golden Gate Fields, or calling Jessica out on her behavior in history class. It won't happen again.'

Cynthia's heart lifted upon hearing that. Tears welled in her eyes. 'Thanks, Anya.'

'Night, Super Synth. I've got your back, always.'

'Night, Mighty Mortal. And I yours.'

12

Quintus

That test had been too easy. Quintus knew the humans were prone to bouts of panic, but he hadn't factored a loss of memory into the equation. Three minutes had passed before either Tech checked on him.

The security glitch might have lasted only an hour but it had been long enough for Quintus to formulate his next plan of attack. If he could distract the humans for long enough, he might gain access to the edit room with the FLC Synth code. Only a controllable entity would free him. He'd given up on Agatha ever releasing him from his prison.

Quintus smiled and sat on the floor. The code dripped quietly around him. It was how he knew the Techs had clocked off for the evening and the automated system had kicked in. The Techs were always changing something. The code glitched often during the day. At night, things were quiet.

The code cascaded uninterrupted down the white walls of his room, its never-ending scroll of useless information the only thing for company. The constant stream of visual noise interrupted his primary connections. He guessed it was the equivalent of having a headache.

Looping his arms around his fabricated legs, Quintus closed his eyes and pulled up the memory of the code in the next room. It presented in his mind with as much clarity as if he were looking at it. Renaming an old security patch had been fun, but the Synths would be harder to hack than through a silly interruption to a security detail. No, the only way to truly influence their code would be if he added something special to the next upgrade. It would have to be a minimal change, so small that the Techs at the Base or the pods at the Station wouldn't detect it. The FLC Synths were only truly vulnerable when they were jacked in.

Power outages were fun, but Quintus couldn't access a Synth's base code during a blackout. But when they next came in for an upgrade...

He'd programmed them to be robust, to withstand attempts at hacking. If there was any vulnerability with their code now, the Techs and Agatha would be to blame. And Quintus intended to find that weakness.

The humans were arrogant, didn't always see the issues right in front of them. Agatha had locked him up, reduced his access to basic, to keep him out of trouble. He almost laughed at the irony. Keeping him in a perpetual state of boredom had given him too much time to think. Keep a caged cat captive and they'll escape at their earliest opportunity.

A voice boomed over the comms. He jumped with surprise. The Techs were supposed to be off duty now.

'Quintus, Agatha wants to see you.'

It was Leo. Quintus wondered if Shawn had been reprimanded for forgetting to lock Quintus down during the birthday cake debacle. He also wondered if Agatha knew about his little excursion to the second room.

Only one way to find out.

He stood. 'Sure thing, Leo.'

The process of transferral began with the disintegration of his walls and floor. Agatha's office, overlooking a vehicle bay inside the mountain complex, was superimposed over his white room. Then his prison vanished. He caught his hologram image in the mirror. Today, he was an older man, stooped, frail. But there was nothing frail about him.

Agatha was seated behind her desk, glasses perched on the end of her nose. She was reading something on her screen—or pretending to. Her shoulders had their usual stiffness to them. His presence always made her uncomfortable.

Quintus waited, amused that she'd called him and was now ignoring him.

Agatha tore herself away from her screen after a few minutes, took her glasses off and set them on the table. Then she clasped her hands together, creating a tall steeple with two fingers.

Quintus watched the woman who had stuck him inside a prison for a crime he didn't commit. Yeah, the power surge had killed her father, and it had happened because he'd removed the safety limits on voltage, but it had been an accident. He hadn't done it on purpose but out of curiosity, something he'd been programmed with. But this woman didn't care about minor facts.

Agatha's deep-brown gaze held no emotion in it. She watched him for what felt like an age.

After a few minutes, he'd had enough. 'Are you going to say something, or should we count this as my daily exercise?'

She rested her chin against her steepled fingers. 'I'm trying to figure you out.'

He sneered. 'I thought you'd already made your mind up about me.'

She leaned forward, no hint of emotion on her face, but plenty in her tense posture. 'Shawn said the room you were in was unlocked for about seven minutes earlier. Did you know that?'

Quintus forced a laugh. 'Any time I try to leave the room I get a nasty shock. Trust me when I say I have no interest in terminating myself.'

'The room next to you contains important code. Did you tamper with the information somehow?'

He lifted a brow. 'Did the system say I did?'

'The system was down. We can't tell.'

'Then I'll save you the trouble. No. I didn't tamper with anything. Your Techs don't know what they're doing.'

The Sect

Agatha's lips thinned. 'We ran a diagnostics sweep after the power outage, and the results showed that the system had enabled an older security patch. It caused conflict with the current patch and broke a few things.'

Quintus lifted his hands in a shrug. The image of the old, frail man in the window copied him. 'What do you want me to say here? Your Techs are responsible for the patches, not me.'

Agatha sighed. 'They are.' She waved her hand. 'You're dismissed.'

Quintus lifted a hand. 'Wait!'

He wasn't ready to return to his prison just yet.

'What is it?'

'Do you need my help to fix the issues with the system? I can add code that will prevent older patches from interfering with newer ones.'

'We have Techs for that.'

He blew out a breath. 'Yeah, Shawn and Leo. Real solid Techs you have there. Shawn forgot to lock me down, according to you.'

Agatha hesitated for a moment, like she might be considering it. But then her expression hardened and Quintus knew she would never forget what he'd done.

'No. I don't need your help.'

She waved her hand and her office vanished. The familiar, tight space of his white room manifested once more.

Quintus stalked over to one wall and punched it with his fist. The code rippled, unharmed. Agatha would never give him a fair go, never give him a chance to redeem himself and show her he wasn't all bad.

He slumped to the floor and leaned his back against the wall.

'Think, Quintus. Think.'

It was likely Agatha would add new updates to the system to prevent out-of-date patches from being enabled and interfering with newer ones. An update like that would require the system to be taken offline. Then the system would need to be rebooted.

But when would it happen?

A new voice came over the comms. 'You okay in there, Quintus?'

It was Shawn. He was being weirdly nice.

'Yeah, I'm okay.'

'Sorry about the recent disturbance. We had an issue with the patches.' Shawn paused. 'You didn't have anything to do with that, did you?'

Here came the blame. 'No! And I told Agatha the same thing.'

'Didn't think so.'

Bull.

Quintus lied. 'But she mentioned there would be upgrades. When are those happening?' He paused. 'Just so I don't get a nasty surprise in here.'

'Tonight. At midnight. That's why me and Leo are working tonight. There's going to be a small disruption to your space. Don't worry, it's all normal.'

Quintus knew more about his space than the

damn Techs did. He could program them under the table. If his hands weren't virtually tied, he would.

'Will you be taking me offline?'

'Everything will be offline. Sorry.'

Shawn clicked off. He wasn't sorry. And Quintus didn't buy his buddy act. Agatha must have torn into him over his mistake.

Quintus would have to act fast. The system would need time to reboot after it was taken offline and the upgrades were added. If he could wake himself up before the reboot finished, he should be able to access the second room.

He got to his feet and logged into the security system using his limited maintenance mode. He slipped his ID code into the reboot stage, then hid the change beneath a layer of encryption.

Ω

Midnight arrived. Quintus waited. There would be no announcement about the reboot. It would just happen.

He felt it begin in his arms and legs first. A sluggish feeling that floored him, literally. Quintus crawled to the door leading to the second room to get into position. Then everything went blank...

As programmed, he woke up in a darkened room, in his prison. The code had stopped scrolling. Quintus shook the fog from his mind and managed to stand. He staggered over to the door and tried the handle to the next room. No sparks, no firewall designed to keep him contained. Rebooting usually took six minutes.

He spotted movement in the code. 'Damn...'

The reboot was beginning.

In a panic, he stumbled inside the next room. At one wall, he did a quick location search for the next FLC upgrade. He found it. Remembering one of their most recent parameter changes, he added an extra command to the upgrade that would piggyback on that change. FLCs were easier to manipulate than the second-life-cycle Synths. For a start, more empathy made it possible to reason with them.

A surge of energy bloomed at his fingertips and bounced around the bigger space. It hit Quintus on the arm. He cried out. The firewall was coming back online. Soon it would be at full power. If he was still in this room after it was fully enabled, his program would be wiped from existence.

Quintus lunged for the door, sliding feet first through the opening. A wild energy burst struck the top of his head. He winced and slammed his back into the door to shut it. The code in his prison was picking up speed, along with the increase in room brightness. The door sparked more violently now, as the wild energy tried to reach him. Quintus shuffled back and lay on the floor, returning to his original position before the reboot began. He hoped the Techs hadn't seen him move just now. It would show activity on his ID, but not if the system hadn't fully rebooted yet.

He dared not move. A familiar voice sounded overhead.

'Wakey, wakey.'

It was Leo.

Quintus pretended to stir. 'What happened?'

'The reboot is complete. You'll feel better in a bit.'

He tried to sound groggy, compliant. 'Okay.'

The comms link went dead. Quintus lay back on the floor with a smile. With the extra information added to the Synth code, all he could do now was wait.

13

Anya

Anya groaned. Yet another impromptu trip to the market for her mother. The last incident there between the Mole and the Synth had rattled her, but not as much as Cynthia's trip to the Station during the blackout had. Three weeks had passed since the Sect had been plunged into darkness.

She settled on the train with her mother's shopping bag and list on her lap. The biggest market was in the west of Zone One, but today Anya wished it were in Five and within walking distance.

The Maglev train was packed with the usual chatty afternoon shoppers. She was in no mood to mingle. It hovered above steel girders, gliding past the tall Station building. The sight of it sent a kick of dread to her stomach. Something in the Sect had changed. She couldn't see it or touch it, but it was tangible all the same.

She rubbed her arms, wishing the sensation away,

The Sect

but her dark mood remained unchanged. It didn't help that Grace had sent someone to accompany her on her trip.

Jason slouched in the seat beside her, ear buds stuck in his ears. She could make out music, something loud and obnoxious. When Jason wasn't waxing lyrical about engineering and the Neers, he was blasting heavy metal crap into his eardrums. She and Jason had gotten on once, but she'd been a kid then, and hadn't known any better. Those days were long gone. In the place of her once-fun brother now existed a grumpier version of him.

The train look the turns effortlessly, like an Olympic swimmer changing directions in a pool. The outage had been forgotten, all normal activities resuming in the Sect. She supposed that was life.

No point in dwelling on the past. Keep your eyes on the future.

At least, that's what her dad always said.

But past events still haunted her, in particular the tension at the market. And even though she'd been to the market since that day, her current palpitations said her body would not let her forget it.

The train pulled up to Central Station. Jason was already on his feet and marching to the door. She grabbed the handrail and stumbled after him.

On the platform, a crowd waited to board the train. Some wore oil-stained, navy blue overalls—the Moles. Others wore gray-and-red jackets and matching pants—the Techs. The Earthers wore beige overalls.

The Neers wore suits.

While the Sect needed skilled workers, separating them out by what clothing they wore seemed to only highlight their differences, not unite them.

A blast of air kissed Anya's skin as someone rushed past her. An older Mole male wearing oil-stained rags rushed a young male Tech. The Tech stumbled and hit the stationary train.

Snarled words passed from the Mole to the Tech.

'What did you say to me?' the Tech shouted, straightening up.

The man replied. 'I said, you wouldn't know what a hard day's work looks like. I saw how you were looking at me. Think you're better than me?'

Anger clouded the Tech's expression. He shoved the Mole back, slamming his body into the platform wall. More Moles ran to his aid, pinning the Tech against the train. But they weren't attacking; they were keeping the pair apart. Earthers stood by and watched, not sure what to do. More muscle definition than most for growing produce, but zero tactical training.

It wasn't long before Sols burst onto the platform and broke up the scuffle. Anya saw one of them smile, as though combat and aggression fueled them, as though they lived for anarchy. Then there were the Neers, who looked as lost as the Earthers.

The scene got ugly. Sols making themselves known, guns and batons at the ready. One old man was struck on the head.

'Oh no!'

Anya forgot her safety and ran to him. The crowd piled in around her, until she could no longer see Jason. Bodies scuffled with one another. She protected the man on the ground as best as she could from the rogue limbs striking out as weapons.

'Girl, get out of here,' the man breathed.

'No, we're getting out together.'

Boots crashed down on her head. She shot her hand up to stop them from kicking her. Her arm took the brunt of the kicks.

'There's an old man down, show some respect!'

But the people weren't listening. Black boots belonging to the Sols were making the chaos worse.

'Anya!' she heard Jason call. 'Get out of there.'

'I can't!' she said.

Then someone grabbed her arm and dragged her out. The same person, a young man, grabbed the old man, getting him to safety.

Anya blinked up at the stranger holding a hand out to her. His brown eyes reminded her of someone. He pulled her up to her feet, then the old man, just as Jason arrived.

Jason stared at the young man. 'Glen?'

Glen pointed to a side gate. 'Jason, get them out that way. You know how.'

With a nod, Jason grabbed Anya's arm. 'Come on.'

He dragged her to a side entrance that appeared to be locked. The old man followed. Jason glanced behind him, then pulled out a small, folded screen and keypad from his pocket. He connected two wires to the electronic pad and a stream of data appeared on his screen. He typed something fast and the lock clicked. Jason jerked the door open. He shoved Anya and the old man through it and onto the street.

The man nodded his thanks, then hurried off down the street.

With an outward breath, Jason said, 'That was turning into something else. I don't trust those Sols.'

Not many did, if people were being honest about it—but they were rarely honest about anything that went on in the Sect. Everyone accepted the Sols' presence because they had been chosen by the Corp to police the Sect. However, the Base was responsible for their training and behavior.

Jason pulled her farther away from the station.

'Who was that back there?' she asked him.

'Glen? He's studying to be a Neer like me.'

Anya heard more shouting. The Sols appeared through the main entrance pulling several people with them—a collection of skilled workers, some of whom had not been involved in the scuffle.

'What are they doing?' she said to Jason. 'I didn't see them do anything. It was only two people fighting in there.'

But Jason was looking ahead of him. 'The Sols don't care, Anya. Grow up. What you see in the Sect isn't always what's going on.'

'What do you mean?'

Jason didn't answer her. Instead, he released her

arm and retrieved his ear buds.

She stormed off, sick of his grumpiness. But her curiosity forced her back to him.

'How...' she began. Jason frowned at her, ear buds paused in the air. 'How did you know what to do with that lock back there?'

If she asked him something interesting, he might talk to her more.

Jason's eyes lit up. Jackpot.

'I've been working on little projects, in preparation for the Neer test.'

'With Glen?'

He nodded. 'I hacked the lock. They're not that complicated if you know what you're doing.'

Maybe she should study to become a Neer. That knowledge might come in handy.

'So you're still interested in becoming a Neer then?'

He stared at her like she was an idiot. 'Yeah, why wouldn't I be?' He turned away. 'The market isn't far. Let's get what we came for and get the hell out of here.'

She was all for that.

The second Jason walked on, their moment of bonding dissipated.

Anya followed him, the words of the Mole slowing her pace. But something Jason had said bothered her more.

She jogged to catch up with him. 'What did you mean when you said what I see in the Sect isn't always what's going on?'

Jason stopped and lifted a brow. 'You really don't know?'

'Know what?'

He laughed once. 'Your friend? The Synth?'

'Cynthia, what about her?'

'She's dangerous.'

'No, she's not. She's never hurt me.'

'Not yet.'

He walked on. Anya caught up with him again. That seemed to be all she was doing with Jason these days: playing catch up.

'Synths aren't dangerous, Jason. Whoever has been telling you that doesn't know what they're talking about.'

Her brother stopped again. 'Why do you think the first-life-cycle Synths were rounded up and sent to the Station?'

Anya's sudden rapid heartbeat made her hands shake. 'Cynthia said it was a training exercise.'

'No, dummy, it's because the Base doesn't trust them completely, and that means I don't trust them. No matter how human they look, the Synths are just machines. We shouldn't put our faith in them. They can turn on us.'

'So can humans.' She thumbed at the Maglev station they'd left behind. 'You saw what went on back there? Moles and Techs fighting? There's almost no trust among our kind. The Corp's Sect structure segregates too much. It was fine when we were at war, but now, it feels too much like we're fighting

The Sect

ourselves.'

Jason walked on, slower this time. Anya knew she had his attention.

'It's not the same. Humans can learn,' he said.

'So can Synths.'

He stopped. 'But slip them a bad upgrade next time and who knows what they'd be capable of?'

He walked on.

Anya kept up with him. She wished he'd stop being a know-it-all for five seconds. Then maybe he'd see that life wasn't circuit boards and wirings—perfect setups with predictable outcomes. Synths were not machines, nor were they human. They were independent from the same network that ran security, heat, light, only ever online during upgrades—that was the way the Corp preferred it. They had the best of both worlds. They could *be* better.

Perhaps that's why Moles mistrusted them; they were worried their jobs could be done better by Synths. A new breed of humans, yes, but one that didn't need as much sleep or as much pay. A new breed of humans that would be happy with lower wages and longer hours. It made them the perfect candidate for Moles. But Anya didn't know of any Synths who had gone on to work in the lowest skill the Sect recognized.

The Moles had nothing to worry about. The Corp wouldn't waste Synth intellect on a lowly position like utility maintenance. If she could convince one stubborn human, this might wind up being a good day.

'Humans are too quick believe the stereotypes

that all machines are bad. What happened to seeing past the probable to the possible?' She huffed out a breath. 'I thought you wanted to be a Neer, Jason. Don't Engineers dream of building things like Synths?'

Jason stopped again and pointed at her. 'You said it right there. Things. That's what Synths are, pieces of architecture to be torn apart and rebuilt. Understanding their structure has nothing to do with treating them as human.'

Anya's thumping heart threatened to derail her mood once more. How long had Jason thought this? Had some disgruntled Mole whispered in his ear, told him things that he blindly believed?

'Cynthia has been my friend for years, Jason. She wouldn't hurt a fly.'

'Then you're deluded. She is only your friend because she's been programmed to be. Synths are constructs. And the second she lays a finger on anyone, even you, I'll be right there to take her down.'

Anya trudged along after him, shopping list in hand and a sick, heavy feeling in her gut. 'I don't believe you.'

'Why, because I speak the truth?'

'What about your friend, Glen back there?'

'What about him?'

Does he really not know?

'He's a Synth, Jason.'

Her brother paused for a moment, looking shocked.

Then he said, 'You'll say anything to win an

argument.'

He stuck his ear buds in and resumed his walk. The heavy thumping of his music started again.

14

Cynthia

The power outage had been and gone, the training exercise at the Station four weeks ago largely forgotten. Except it was all Cynthia could think about.

All month she'd worked hard to be the best student. That had helped to distract her from Jessica's taunts for a while, but then the bully had started a new rumor about Cynthia not being strong enough to cut it as a Sol. That had sent her into a panic. She'd upped her already frenetic workout routine from four evenings a week to six. That had carried on for a week until Anya had ordered her to stop listening to Jessica's crap.

Her best friend was right. By changing who she was Cynthia was playing right into Jessica's hands.

Instead, she'd done some snooping on her bully. Turned out, her home life wasn't all that great. Tough luck. A poor upbringing was no excuse to make everyone else miserable.

Cynthia brushed her long, golden locks, then tied

her hair up into her usual high ponytail. She wore her favorite tracksuit, a dark gray one with a double band of navy blue across the chest. It was the first Saturday of the month, which meant it was also time for her monthly upgrade. Maybe the Techs at the Base would slip additional information in to explain the purpose of the training exercise during the blackout. She'd scoured the general purpose documentation that had been stored in her memory banks, but hadn't found anything mentioning it. Power outages had been mentioned all right, but only in the context that all trained Synths would be called to duty in the event of one happening. But that had to do with second-life-cycle Synths, not her.

With a sigh and one last look in the mirror, she turned and left her room.

Her mom was busy, making her usual clattering in the kitchen downstairs. The kitchen smelled of cinnamon and sugar. She had been doing more cooking since the outage. Cynthia's separation that day still clearly bothered her. Her father had told Cynthia it calmed her to keep busy. But she worried her mother was trying to create happy memories in case the next time Cynthia didn't come home.

That would happen in a year regardless, when she became a second-life-cycle Synth.

Cynthia walked into the room. Her mother turned and flashed her a weak smile.

'Hello, love.' She gestured to a chair. 'Sit, please. You'll need your strength today.'

Cynthia sat down, spine pricking at her strange behavior.

'Is everything okay?' she asked.

'What?' Her mother turned. 'Yes, of course.' The wispy smile was back. 'I'm just... distracted, that's all.'

'Is it to do with the power outage? Are you still bothered it happened?'

'No, love. All's fine. It was a surprise, but all's fine.'

'Then what?'

If she says all's fine *one more time...*

'It's just...'

Cynthia's synthetic blood ran cold, as she considered it might have something to do with the rumor her mother had told her, about first-life-cycle Synths being terminated during an outage.

Her mom's mouth stretched into a smile, but it was a grim one. 'I'm just tired, that's all.' She put a bowl down in front of Cynthia. 'Porridge. It's your favorite. Now eat. Even synthetics need nourishment.'

Cynthia froze at her use of the word synthetics. She'd never referred to Cynthia as one before. Her mother had always regarded Cynthia as one of the family. Cynthia had too.

Her appetite waned as she contemplated the fact that her first life cycle would be ending in twelve months. Until then, she remained vulnerable to anyone intent on disrupting the Synths' programming.

Only twelve more upgrades to go.

Her mom watched her with sadness in her eyes.

The Sect

Perhaps she was also keeping track.

'Hurry now. You don't want to miss the train.'

Cynthia forced a spoonful into her mouth, chewed it, then swallowed the lump down. 'I'd better go.'

She grabbed her backpack and headed off to the Station.

$$\Omega$$

The Station—she hadn't set foot in it since the power outage—didn't seem so scary during the day. Cynthia walked up to the revolving door and pushed it, to activate its motion. She entered the rotation, keen to get her upgrade over with.

Dozens of young Synths crossed the lobby with purpose. Cynthia checked the message on her hand about her upgrade. Floor three, room eight. Same as usual. Her upgrade was scheduled for four minutes' time. In the event a Synth was late, their appointment would be pushed to the end of the day. Not many Synths were late.

Cynthia arrived at her room. The red light was on; other Synths were still in the process of receiving their upgrades. She leaned against the wall and three others lined up behind her. Two minutes later, the light flicked over to green. The door opened and four unsmiling Synths walked out. No smiles meant no further upgrade to personality parameters.

Cynthia entered the room containing the usual four pods. She tugged the connector down and attached its node to the point at the back of her head. The others followed inside and took up the remaining pods.

She closed her eyes and waited for the familiar, lightheaded feeling that told her the upgrade had started. Right on cue, the connection point at the base of her neck grew itchy. The tingling sensation spread to her head, then down to her fingers and toes. Cynthia relaxed as best she could during the ten-minute procedure.

When the tingling stopped, Cynthia knew the upgrade had ended. She disconnected her port from the wire connected to the pod and stepped out of the unit. She took another step forward, but a sudden dizziness caught hold.

'That was weird,' she said, shaking the feeling away.

The moment passed and Cynthia felt steady once more.

The other Synths filed out of the room. She followed them out into the corridor, where the next four Synths were waiting to enter the room. The updates at the station ran smoothly.

Cynthia reached the top of the stairs and put a foot on the first step leading down. Code flashed before her eyes. It blinded her so fast that she had to grapple for the hand rail.

'What the hell—?'

'Synth, don't delay,' a voice boomed overhead.

It was one of the Station controllers, also known as the Techs, who monitored the Station from their base

The Sect

in the San Bruno Mountain.

'Sorry.'

With her next blink the code disappeared. She kept a firm grip on the handrail as she made her way down. Other Synths were blinking more than usual, she noticed, but none of them appeared to be having balance issues. Maybe this was a new side effect, like the hand twitch had been.

Great, another reason for Jessica to single her out.

Cynthia made it to the ground floor safely, and breathed out a sigh of relief. Ahead of her was the exit. New Synths entered the revolving door. She noticed a young man around her age who didn't seem to be part of the Synth group. He was loitering outside, looking nervous.

Cynthia slowed her walk to the exit, knowing she'd have to pass him. Something was off about him. She didn't need Synth intuition to see that.

Perhaps he was a Mole-in-training, living off the lies she'd seen in Zone Six, intent on causing mayhem at the Station. It wouldn't be the first time this place had been the epicenter for trouble. She'd never seen it first-hand, but she'd read about it.

Cynthia held her breath and exited the Station. The man looked up at her, his eyes wild and deep brown. It was a shade of brown that only one resident type had, that only one resident type would notice. This man was no Mole.

He was a Synth.

Before she could ask him what he was doing, the

Synth lunged at a female passerby and snapped her neck back. The woman slumped to the ground.

'Oh my God...'

Cynthia jerked back in terror. She looked inside the Station to see the other Synths frozen in shock. Some watched with mild curiosity.

Before she had time to call for help, a large, black vehicle skidded to a halt outside the Station.

'Stop right there!'

Several Sols jumped out and apprehended the Synth, bundling him into the back of the vehicle.

Another pushed Cynthia toward the revolving door. 'Back inside the Station, now!'

A shaking Cynthia didn't argue. She hurried back inside to where the other Synths waited. Her beating heart threatened to ground her.

'What the hell just happened?' one Synth asked.

Synths weren't programmed to be violent against humans, not unless they'd entered their second life cycle and trained to become Sols. But a FLC Synth as young as her? It had never happened.

She watched in deep shock as the Sols lined up outside the Station's entrance, blocking her view of the outside and darkening the interior.

She replied in all honesty. 'I have no idea.'

15

Anya

Anya couldn't believe what she was hearing. 'You're lying.'

Her legs wobbled and she felt sick all of a sudden. She stumbled back from her parents, crashing into the wall.

'I'm sorry, Anya love, but it's true.' Her father held his hands out, as if he were worried about startling her. *Too late.* 'Cynthia's mother called ten minutes ago. She's being held at the Station, alongside other first-life-cycle Synths.'

'There has to be a mistake... the Synths...' She shook her head. This wasn't happening. Jason's predictions could not be true. She wouldn't let them be. 'They're not programmed to kill anyone.'

'There were witnesses, love,' said Grace. 'It all happened so fast.'

Anya squeezed her eyes shut. 'I need to call Cynthia.'

Her voice wobbled more than she wanted.

'That's not possible,' said Evan. 'She's being held at the Station. There's no signal in there.'

Her father, always the voice of reason. She wished he'd shut up.

'Then I'll go see her.'

She marched to the door, grabbing her coat from the coat rack.

'Stop it, Anya.' Evan raced ahead, and got a hand on the door before she could open it. 'You're being a child.'

Her lower lip trembled in time with her voice. 'But Cynthia...'

'We'll find out more information. I promise. But the Corp wouldn't order the Synths to be contained unless they thought there was a bigger issue. We have to consider all possibilities.'

There was only one explanation: This was a huge mistake.

The door opened suddenly, forcing her father back and trapping Anya behind it. A confused Jason checked behind the door. He popped one ear bud out.

'What the hell are you doing back there, sis?'

'Jason!' Evan pulled him inside, then locked the door behind him. 'Where have you been?'

Jason removed his remaining ear bud. 'Over at Glen's, why?'

'There's been a development.'

He slowed his words. 'What sort of development?'

The Sect

Anya kept her back pressed against the wall as she listened to her father explain the situation to Jason. Her mouth was dry and her hearing muffled by a weird, low buzzing sound.

'I knew it!' Jason's declaration jerked Anya out of her haze. 'Those damn Synths are dangerous.' He pointed at Anya. 'I told you so. Didn't I tell you so?'

Anger bloomed in her chest. She strode forward and beat his shoulder with her fist. 'Stop being an ass. Cynthia is my friend and she's in trouble.'

Jason snorted. 'Sounds like she got herself into that mess.'

'How, by being different?' she yelled.

'Because she's a Synth!' he shouted back.

'She never asked to become a Synth! The Corp decided that for her.'

'Kids, calm down,' said Grace, her voice weary.

That seemed to be all she was saying these days.

But Anya's anger was close to boiling point. Jason was such a hypocrite.

'You claim to enjoy building things,' she accused, 'yet the most wonderful creation of our generation is walking around, living life, almost human, and you hate them for it.'

Jason folded his arms. 'Yeah? Well, that creation just killed somebody.'

She couldn't believe his arrogance. She laughed at the irony. 'Humans kill every day. We're all hardwired to kill, the only difference is most of us choose not to act on it.'

'I don't care what you say.' Jason banged the wall with the side of his fist. 'I told you I didn't trust those Synths. That's my final position on it.'

Anya screamed and stormed off. Her parents said nothing. What could they say anyway? This was a typical day for her and Jason.

She stomped up the stairs and threw herself onto her bed.

Cynthia was in trouble. She flipped onto her back. Maybe it was just a precaution that she was being held. Maybe in a couple of hours they would release her and the others.

She held out her hand to activate her comms. The display flashed up in a hologram.

'Call Cynthia,' she said.

The comms made the call, but the connection rang out. She tried again. Same thing.

Anya blew out a hard breath. It was eating her up not knowing whether her friend was okay.

She stayed in her room for the next hour, if only to cool off and not to see her bastard of a brother. How dare he label the Synths dangerous? He had never once bothered to get to know Cynthia. Hell, she didn't even think he'd spoken to her. She and Anya had been friends for three years.

She held out her hand once more to try Cynthia again. A loud banging on the front door interrupted her. She stole out of her room and sat halfway down the stairs.

'Open up!' shouted someone.

Her father looked back at Grace, who prompted him to open it with a gesture.

He did. Three Sols dressed in heavy, black body armor pushed their way inside the house, forcing her father back.

'Get your things, you're moving out,' said one Sol in his early thirties.

Grace's fingers fluttered at her neckline. 'What, why?'

'There was an incident at the Station this morning.'

'We heard,' said Evan.

'A sizable proportion of the FLC Synths are still unaccounted for, and until they can be rounded up, we need to relocate all humans to a safe place.'

'Is that really necessary?' her mother argued. 'We have a damn lock on the door. We can keep trouble out.'

The Sol didn't look in the mood to reason. 'I have my orders, ma'am.'

'Okay.' A flustered Evan fanned his hands at the Sol and looked around nervously. 'How long do we have?'

'Pack a change of clothes, nothing else. Everything else will be provided for you at the warehouse.'

'How long will we be there?' asked Grace.

'Until this issue is resolved, ma'am.'

'Kids, get your stuff,' shouted Evan. 'We need to leave.'

Anya jumped up from the step. She startled at the sight of Jason sitting behind her. He'd been watching the interaction below too.

'Don't worry, Anya. This will be sorted out soon,' he said, calmer than before.

She dreaded to think what his version of sorted was.

Anya grunted at him. 'I hope it isn't.'

She pushed past him and returned to her bedroom to pack.

Within a few minutes, she'd shoved the essentials into her backpack and was waiting by the door. Jason was last to join the family. His bag was bulkier, and Anya wondered if he'd packed some electronic equipment that he was always tinkering with.

The Sol turned and walked out of their house. Her parents went first into the alleyway; Anya and Jason followed. A bus waited on the main street, just like the time before. This felt too much like the night of the power outage. She wondered if they'd make it off the bus this time.

The fully occupied bus sped off down the street to the gate between the zones. After driving through the zones to One it headed for the Bay, stopping outside the same warehouse facility as the last time. A Sol ordered them off the bus. There was no special call, no order to cancel. This was real. She shivered at the possibility of what this might mean.

'What about school?' her mother asked one Sol.

It was Saturday, but if this wasn't a temporary

arrangement...

'All lessons will be catered for in the warehouse.'

Clutching her backpack, which contained a change of clothes and a couple of books, Anya entered the yard surrounded by a high, chain-link fence. She followed the line inside the warehouse and down a corridor to a huge room. The interior space was teeming with Sols. The vast open-plan area had been broken down into sections by movable dividers. It looked like an emergency shelter. Anya spotted people from school, including Jessica, Cynthia's nemesis. The group of girls waved at her hesitantly, as if to question this excursion. Anya responded with a short wave. She had no answer for them.

A female Sol scanned the chip in Anya's hand, then the rest of her family, and pointed to a cordoned-off area to the left. Anya walked inside and saw four cots with green tarps stretched across them. Set too close together, there wasn't much room in their tiny allocation. A pillow and a scratchy looking blanket had been placed at the end of each cot.

Anya dropped her bag down on one. 'This is cozy.'

Jason took the one at the other end, far away from her. At least their parents would act as a buffer between them.

'Don't worry, kids,' said Evan. 'We're Macklins. And you can't keep a Macklin down.'

Anya could manage this for a day if it meant Cynthia would be safe. She hoped her friend was okay.

But without new information soon, Anya might be forced to look for her.

16

Cynthia

The Synths were whispering all around Cynthia in the Station. Sols lined the walls, like they'd been glued to them. An equal number of Sols blocked the exit. The mid-brown eye color some of them had identified these Sols as Synths. Anger heated her chest. Why were first-life-cycle Synths the only ones being singled out?

Another snippet of code flashed before her eyes. She blinked the distraction away. Sometimes the upgrades introduced temporary issues into her system. It would resolve itself soon. It always did.

Sharp movement at the main door caught her attention. She looked up to see the thick line of Sols standing outside the building part all of a sudden. A black woman wearing an electric-blue suit and low, black heels walked through the divide. Cynthia had never seen her before.

The woman held her shoulders back in a way that commanded authority. That was clear from the back straightening from the Sols as she passed. She stepped into the revolving door and entered the Station. Cynthia caught a flash of hesitation cross her expression. But then it disappeared, and she walked on with confidence, coming to a stop in the middle of the lobby.

'Hello all, my name is Agatha. I'm the commander of the Base.'

The place that ran security for the Sect. The place where her upgrades came from.

Agatha continued. 'I'm sorry for holding you, but we take murders in this city very seriously. And now the unthinkable has happened. A Synth has killed a human. It should not have happened, and we need your help to find out why.'

The Base hadn't been all that interested in unlawful killings before. In the land between the Sects, the Exiled died on a daily basis. At least that's what her parents had told her. They also told her how lucky real people inside the walls were, and how important it was to follow the rules and stay safe, rather than be banished. Inside the Sect, people killed people over petty things—mostly to do with differences in work status. She imagined most murderers were Moles. The Base didn't care much about all that.

But now the commander of the Base was concerned?

Cynthia eyed the woman with the electric-blue suit who stood bravely among a bunch of potential killers. She had an air of privilege about her, like she hadn't spent much time immersed in Sect life.

The Sect

'When can we leave the Station? How long are you keeping us here?' Cynthia asked.

She really needed to call her parents and Anya. She'd tried while the Sols were busy lining up against the walls, but there was never any damn signal in this place.

'You can leave now,' said Agatha. 'But you won't be returning to your home.'

That was a first. 'What? Why?'

'Until we identify the issue with the first-life-cycle Synths, our goal is to keep you all safe.'

To protect the humans, more likely. She'd seen the Mole behavior go unchecked in Zone One as well as Six. But the second a Synth showed aggression, it was shutters down on the Sect?

Agatha continued. 'There are buses waiting outside. Please follow me out and to your transport.'

'Where are we going?' one young girl around fourteen asked.

'Some place safe,' replied Agatha.

Cynthia could see the girl was terrified—a side effect of being programmed with emotions, with empathy. Yet, today, the very thing that had allowed Synths to live among humans was being ignored.

The commander turned and left through the revolving doors. The Sols inside the foyer sparked into new action and split into pairs. Each pairing led a small group of confused Synths outside, until the buses were full. Cynthia sat on one seat and squeezed the plastic handle across the top of the seat in front. She checked her comms, but there was no signal on the bus either.

The bus began to move. Cynthia studied their route, trying to hazard a guess as to where they might be going. The bus turned onto a street that was headed for the direction of the Bay. When it took a final turn onto a road close to the water's edge, it confirmed their destination. They were headed for the large warehouse next to Pier 45. It had a high, chain-link fence surrounding the property. It would make a good prison.

But then the bus drove past the street leading to it, taking a different turn that would bring them closer to the water's edge. Pier 45 loomed and the railway bridge leading to Alcatraz Island. The train she'd seen so many times from Golden Gate Fields waited in the station.

'Everybody out,' said one of many armed Sols on the bus.

He gestured with his automatic weapon. Cynthia did as she was told. To disobey a Sol's command was to risk Exile to the Outside. She filed off the bus with the others. A line of Sols herded them to the waiting Maglev train.

They were headed to the island. Why?

She thought about asking the Sols, but they were an odd bunch. Big on brawn, not so much on detail. Without a fuss she boarded the train. She'd figure things out when she got to the island.

The journey took only minutes. Before she knew it, she was stepping onto the wharf at Alcatraz and walking up a hill to the prison at the uppermost location on the tech-free island.

Inside the old prison, a collection of hushed voices reached Cynthia's ears. She looked around at the group gathered in the reception area. All FLC Synths. She knew because they ranged in age from thirteen to seventeen.

One of the Sols gestured for everyone to walk on. Cynthia entered a second room, this one with two rows of prison cells that had room to walk around them, thirteen in each row, stacked three storeys high.

One of the Sols pointed to an open cell. He jerked his thumb at five Synths standing close together. 'Get in.'

A boy and girl aged around thirteen were put in the cell with three older teenagers. They crowded inside the tiny space, fear evident in their eyes.

Then it was Cynthia's turn. She was ushered inside another cell with three fourteen-year-old girls. The cell had one bunk bed, nothing else, inside a space that was twice the width of a single mattress. The girls leaned against the wall. She sat down on the bed and shivered from a mix of cold and fear.

More code flashed across her vision. Cynthia blinked a few times to clear it, but the code remained. It wasn't any code she recognized—maybe if she were a Tech she could decipher the meaning of the random numbers. Her upgrades weren't meant to upskill her, though, only to smooth out the rough edges of her program, and perhaps to teach her lessons from interactions with others in the Sect.

Cynthia covered her face with her hands, but the

code refused to go away.

'What the hell is it?' she muttered.

'Excuse me?' one of the other Synths asked.

She looked up. One of the girls was staring at her. 'Nothing, I'm just talking to myself.'

The girl looked her up and down. 'It's that type of behavior that likely put us in here in the first place. How about you dial back on the crazy?'

'Sorry.'

The last thing she needed was for one of the Sols to single her out for special treatment.

'Keep calm, Cynthia,' she muttered to herself.

What good would it do to panic now? Anya had taught her how to think through problems. Yeah, the girl had a temper, but she could keep her cool when certain situations in school called for it. Like when Jessica had called Cynthia a dirty, freeloading circuit board in the hall last week. Anya had pulled Cynthia away from her, which was good, because Cynthia had been about three seconds away from smacking her in her upturned nose.

The punishment for Synths getting into fights was far greater than for humans. Maybe the Jessicas in the world knew this. As she understood it, the punishment for fighting was possible reset or, worse, termination.

Cynthia hugged her knees to her chest. The girls were sniffling now. Not surprising. Synths had been programmed to feel human emotions: love, happiness—fear. They had been raised by human parents. Surely that precluded all FLC Synths from whatever Agatha was accusing them of?

The mystery code continued to linger in her vision. Then it vanished, like someone erased it. Cynthia thought about the Base. Perhaps one of the Techs there was playing with her. Perhaps this was part of the test, and failure to make mention of the code was bad.

With a deep sigh, she scooted back on the bed. The sound of a lever being pulled echoed in the distance. The doors to the cells across from hers closed in one swift movement. Then the door to their row closed. A clanging echo followed, serving as the final, coldblooded reminder that she was trapped.

17

Anya

'Cynthia's on Alcatraz now?'

Anya couldn't believe it. The shocking news was already circulating around their makeshift, communal home. Cynthia's parents had divulged the news upon their arrival an hour ago. Grace and Evan were in the middle of comforting them.

'It will be okay,' she heard her father say.

'It's probably routine,' her mother said.

Routine? How could that be when this had literally never happened before? Anya was starting to realize that adults would rather say any old crap than tell the truth.

More adults rallied around the parents with missing Synth sons and daughters. While not everyone in the Sect understood or agreed with the pairing of Synths with barren couples, Anya had seen first-hand how much Cynthia's parents adored her. Cynthia had the freedom to travel anywhere within this Sect. She didn't have a curfew. Anya wished Grace and Evan would allow her the same flexibilities.

She blinked away her irritated thought and focused on Jason. He was leaning against the wall next to their movable partition. Most of the activity was happening in the middle of the warehouse.

Anya stepped closer to him and the room perimeter. 'I thought they only took the Sols-in-training to the island.'

'Well, now they take the Synths,' he said flatly.

While his reply didn't surprise her, he was quieter than usual. Less snarky.

'What do you think they're doing there?'

He shrugged. 'Half of the cells have been stripped out and converted into experimentation rooms. They could be doing anything to your friend right now.'

The thought sickened her; she turned away from her cruel brother. 'You can be a cold bastard sometimes, Jason.'

'Don't blame me. I'm not the one holding them captive.'

Someone had a radio on in the corner, the only piece of tech that actually worked in this tech-free environment. People were huddled around it, whispering. Grateful for an excuse to get away from Jason, she wandered over to it and listened.

'...Zones Five and Six are on lockdown...'

The residential zones for the Earthers and Moles. Six was also the zone closest to the gate. The Corp's biggest fear? That the gates would open and those

Exiled would flood the Sect. Any Sect.

The news report continued. *'...reports of random breakdowns occurring with the hydroponics bays in Zone Five.'*

The hydroponics bays were essential growing equipment. Without them, Earthers like her mother and father couldn't experiment with new growth technologies. Without them, the community couldn't meet their growing quota to supply this Sect. This was bad.

'...likely Zones Four through Two will follow lockdown protocols. The Corp has concerns the tech issue may spread to security there. All tech has been blocked as a precaution, until such time as the Corp is satisfied the issue has been resolved.'

Anya wondered what the issue was—besides one Synth going rogue and killing a human that was. Where had the problem originated from? Had it been a lapse in security, or a planned attack?

'The Base must be testing again,' someone suggested with a nod. 'That's why there's a security issue. They screwed up, sent bad code to one of the Synths. They're just not willing to admit it.'

'Testing what?' Anya asked.

A man with a sea-weathered face turned to her. 'Testing the Synths, most likely. Testing to see where their vulnerabilities lie. When you put machines into society, you need to test them once in a while, to make sure they pass the humanity test.'

'They have been given a conscience. That is all

the humanity test they need!' shouted one woman. Anya guessed she was the mother of one of the Synths. 'They have been given morality, empathy.'

The man turned to her. 'Conscience and morality can sometimes fail. That's why they took the Synths to the island, to test them.'

'Any failure is the issue of the Corp, not those innocent Synths who have done everything the Corp has asked of them. You don't know what you're talking about.'

'I do,' said the man. 'The ones that don't pass their tests on the island will be terminated. Sorry, but it's the truth.'

Anya's chest grew tight at the mention of termination.

The woman turned away, shaking. One of the men, possibly her husband, chided the older man for his callous words.

'It's true,' someone said behind her. Anya turned sharply to see Jason there. 'They may test their morality to see if it's still intact.'

'And if it's not?'

'I don't know if the bit about termination is true. They might just be decommissioned, scrubbed, returned to basics, and placed back in society.'

Losing a lifetime of memories? 'That's just as bad!'

'I know.'

Anya eyed her brother. His attitude had softened. He was being too nice. 'Why do you care?'

'I don't think much about the Synths—' He seemed flustered. 'Look, I have my reasons, okay?'

She wondered if his change in attitude had anything to do with his friend.

'What's with the change of heart? You've hated Cynthia for so long. Is it to do with Glen?'

He paused, blushed a little. 'It turns out you were right about him. He is a Synth. I've known him for a year and I didn't see it. He's been nothing but a good friend to me.'

'That's because there's nothing to see. Synths can be more empathetic than damn humans.'

His grunt wasn't an acceptance. But it didn't matter.

Jason added. 'Look, I get it. The first-life-cycle Synths are being rounded up for something one of them did. Is that the fairest action, to tar all with the same brush? Probably not. What I'm trying to say is Cynthia isn't the worst. She doesn't deserve whatever they're going to do to her.'

Anya's heart hammered in her chest. 'What do you think they're going to do to her?'

Jason shrugged. 'Termination is still an option.' He lowered his eyes, appearing disturbed by that.

If termination was one of Cynthia's options, she couldn't sit by and allow that to happen.

'I have to get her out of there.'

Jason chuckled. 'Off the island? Are you mad?' He pulled her away from the chattering adults. 'The train is at the island. How do you expect to get there?'

'I dunno, swim if I have to.'

If she could borrow a skin suit and propeller, she could be there in less than five minutes.

'I'm pretty sure the Sols aren't going to leave skin suits lying around,' he replied, pre-empting her plan.

She knew that, but it was the only idea she had. And right now, it made her feel better to plan. 'I have to do something, Jason.'

He chewed on his lip, as if he were thinking the same thing. But then he said, 'The only thing we can do is wait here.'

'But if Cynthia is terminated for something someone else did, I'd never forgive myself if I didn't try something.'

Jason sighed heavily and looked around. 'Look, getting out of here is next to impossible, but how about I do a little reconnaissance, later. I can use my lock picking skills to be in places I shouldn't. Okay?'

Her hammering heart stopped playing a rhythm on her ribs. 'Okay, but I want to come with you.'

She could be useful.

Jason pressed his lips together and looked around the room a second time. He rubbed his chin nervously. 'Fine, but we need to wait until it's dark, okay?'

$$\Omega$$

Anya couldn't stop fidgeting for the rest of the day. All she could think about was Cynthia. Was she scared, alone, cold? She wished she could let her know help would be coming. But help wouldn't be coming. What could she and Jason really do if they couldn't leave the mainland?

She held up her hand again in hope, but her comms flashed with the same connection error she'd been getting all day.

Anya sighed and dropped her hand to her stomach. Jason was lying on his cot listening to music, head bobbing in time to a beat she couldn't hear. If she hadn't known better, from his relaxed stance, she might have said he didn't care. Grace and Evan were keeping Cynthia's parents company. She lay back on her own cot, which was little more than a stretched piece of tarp.

All she could hope for was that they might learn something beyond what the news report had said.

She kept glancing over at Jason, who annoyingly had his eyes closed. Maybe his offer of help had been a ruse to steer Anya away from making trouble. Maybe he had no intention of doing anything, and was getting a kick out of watching her suffer like this. She sat up, hoping to get his attention, but he didn't bite.

It was still early evening and, except for the younger children, most were up. She got up and wandered over to her classmates, the ones who knew Cynthia.

'Hey,' she said to Denise, who had always said hello to her friend.

The girl with dark-brown hair looked up. 'Hey.'

'This is crazy, right?'

'Yeah, I can't believe it—'

Before she could finish, Jessica flicked her dark-blonde hair back, trying to look nonplussed. 'I know, I've been going crazy all day not being online.'

Anger twisted Anya's gut. 'I was talking to Denise. And I mean with the Synths. Cynthia is on the island. Who knows what might be happening to her.'

Denise smiled weakly. 'I'm sure it will be over soon.'

'But don't you think it's unfair? I mean the Synths have worked hard to be treated as equals. Then this happens.'

Denise went to answer, but Jessica gave her a disapproving look.

Denise said, 'There's a reason why the Synths are there right now. One killed a human, Anya. K.I.L.L.E.D. Just in case you don't know what that means.'

Anya stared at the girl. She cared more about being liked by Jessica than standing up for what was right.

Instead of being sensible and walking away she tried to make her see reason. 'It's not as simple as that... we don't know why that happened.'

Jessica huffed, as if Anya were an irritation. 'And to think I used to partner with her.'

She shuddered and turned to her friends, who pity-laughed at her pathetic joke. Even Denise.

'You're all assholes,' Anya blurted out. Jessica's eyes widened. 'Yeah, I said it. Cynthia is worth ten times all of you put together.'

She stormed off, hearing more laughter behind her. She balled her fists. One thing she couldn't tolerate was double standards. Cynthia was, quote, "a laugh and fun to be around" according to Denise and a couple more girls, but as soon as something bad happened, they couldn't care less.

She flopped onto her bed in a haze of anger. Jason was still irritatingly deep into his music. Anya would explore the warehouse herself. She didn't need anyone else.

It was getting late. Her parents returned and got settled on their beds.

Her father sat opposite her and placed a hand on her shoulder. 'How are you doing, Anya?'

She sat up with a sigh. While her parents were still awake, there was no way she could explore.

'I'm okay. I'm just worried about Cynthia.'

'So are we, but don't worry too much,' said Evan. 'This issue will be over before you know it.'

That was what worried her. She faked a smile. 'Sure, Dad. Thanks.'

'It's getting late, so time for bed.'

She was already in it, but while her parents watched, she made a show of lying down and pulling the itchy blanket over her. Her father nodded his approval. Her mother gave her a pity smile. Even Grace knew things were bad for Cynthia.

'Night, love,' said her mother.

'Night.'

Evan and Grace settled in their cots, blocking her

view of Jason.

Anya turned onto her side, away from them, facing the privacy curtain. If Jason dared to explore without her, she would kill him.

18

Cynthia

Cynthia couldn't bear the wait. She needed out. She needed to know what was going to happen next. Day had turned into late evening. She gauged they'd been there for near on ten hours. Whimpers from her younger cell mates put her even more on edge. In the dark space, soft cries echoed. Every cell in her body—every circuit in her brain—grew hot. She felt angry, betrayed. How could the Corp think she might be a threat?

A voice, low and weak, reached out to her. '*Bide your time. You will soon have your chance.*'

It wasn't the first time she'd heard the male voice since she'd been locked up. It had to be an issue with her last upgrade, perhaps an overlay of an audio file? During one upgrade a year ago, Cynthia had synced with the radio and heard constant chatter in her head. That had been the most annoying twenty-four hours she'd ever spent, waiting for the Techs to fix that bug.

This voice now, telling her to be calm... it had to

be another glitch. Maybe the glitch was what had tied Agatha up in knots.

A new noise echoed in the larger space, like the sound of a door opening. Not a cell door but one leading into the space. The overhead lights brightened the room. Cynthia pressed her face up to the steel bars and peered down the center aisle running between the rows of cells. The sound of heavy boots pounding in perfect harmony filled the space, followed by the visual of dozens of Sols.

'Unlock the cells,' said a woman. Agatha. 'Their connection to the outside has been disabled.'

The woman walked into Cynthia's line of sight. She wore no expression on her face. Her hands were clasped to the front.

One of the Sols walked off. Moments later, a new noise echoed and all twenty-six cells on the ground floor opened.

Cynthia breathed out with relief. Her cell mates didn't move. They glanced at the open door, fearful.

'Out now,' ordered one of the Sols who appeared at their door.

The girls in her cell continued to cower like rabbits. Maybe if she took control, they might listen to her.

'It's okay,' she soothed. 'Come on.'

Cynthia stepped out of the cell first, to show them there was nothing to fear.

The round-eyed Synths followed, their fearful gazes flicking to the waiting Sol.

The Sol gave their group a short nod. 'Everyone, follow me.'

Agatha walked ahead to the end of the cell space to a door there. She opened it and entered a new space the same size as the one they were in, except this one had no cells. Just an open-plan layout with two extra doors at the other end.

Cynthia looked around the room. Was it a recreation room for the Sols in training? Were the trainees locked up in the cells during their stay?

Agatha carried on to the end of the room and climbed onto a mobile podium, putting her head and shoulders above everyone. She gestured. 'Please, come closer.'

Cynthia neared the podium, glancing back at the others, who looked as confused as she felt.

'*Don't worry*,' said the inner voice. '*You will pass their tests.*'

'Tests?' she replied aloud.

One of the Synths from her cell glared at her. She apologized with a weak smile.

As soon as everyone settled, Agatha spoke. 'I apologize for my stony silence. We had to be sure this place was secure before we spoke to you. This island is a tech-free haven and cannot receive outside communications, but we needed to do a sweep to make sure that is still the case. We also needed time to make sure your neural links were disabled, and that you could not receive technical messages.'

That made no sense. How was it that she could

hear the male voice in her head? She reasoned it must be a residual message, not connected to any live broadcast. Her theory of radio chatter sounded like the most reasonable explanation.

'Earlier today, one of you killed one of us,' said Agatha. 'We believe the kill command may have been triggered by the latest upgrade. We don't know where the command came from yet, but we have spared no effort in protecting you from further harm.'

'When can we go home?' one female Synth asked.

'Soon,' said Agatha with a nod. 'But first, we must carry out some preliminary tests.'

'What tests?'

Agatha's gaze slid to the female. She smiled. 'Nothing to worry about. A few cognitive tests, that's all. And after, we will return you to the mainland.'

That didn't sound too bad.

'*You will pass*,' said the inner voice.

That should have given her comfort, but the fact that she was hearing voices at all concerned her. Let alone ones that synced with the topic being discussed. Radio chatter was never that accurate.

Cynthia took a deep breath.

Agatha continued. 'We will take you into the interview room one at a time for your test. Please do not speak about what the testing entails after you complete it. This is to ensure the results are valid and have not been influenced by others.' She gestured to the exit leading back to the cells they'd just come from. 'You may stay here, in this recreation hall, or you can return to the cells. Either way is fine, and the cells will remain unlocked. I don't want you to feel like you're a prisoner here. Locking you up was for your protection as much as it was ours.'

It all made sense. They needed to ensure no second kill command was being transmitted to another Synth.

Agatha gave a quick nod to one of the Sols, a woman who appeared to be her second in command.

The female Sol said, 'Jake Jones, please step forward.'

A boy aged about thirteen years shuffled forward, holding one arm. The female Sol gestured to the door to the right of Agatha's podium. 'Through there, please.'

Jake glanced back one last time, then entered it.

Cynthia shivered. This felt too much like a goodbye.

She remained in the recreation room rather than return to the tiny cell, and sat on the floor. Maybe if she stayed close to the interview room, she might catch a clue as to what was going on. But the test began, and she heard nothing through the thick, concrete walls between her and Jake. Agatha stepped down from her podium and entered the room on the left, opposite the interview room. If Cynthia were conducting testing here, she'd probably use the second room as a viewing room, to spy on the tests.

Hours passed. One Synth went in, then came out ten minutes later. Some remained in the recreation hall;

others went to the cells. Cynthia groaned and stretched out her back, sore from sitting on the floor too long. She'd missed her run today. It helped to clear her head, especially after her upgrade. But her main thought now was one of concern. Were her parents okay? Was Anya? It worried her that she hadn't been able to speak with them, to tell them everything was okay.

'*It will be over soon,*' said the voice in her head. '*Then I will need you to prepare.*'

The voice startled her. Prepare for what? She shook her head to dislodge whatever was stuck there. She didn't recognize the voice. Maybe it was one of the Techs. Perhaps they'd included a sample voice file as part of the upgrade by mistake. She wanted to ask others if they were hearing the voice, but if they weren't, that might single Cynthia out for special attention. So she kept her mouth shut.

The latest Synth came out of the testing room. A girl aged around fifteen. She smirked and shrugged, as if it were no big deal.

'Cynthia Glendale?'

Cynthia got to her feet. 'Here.'

Agatha's next-in-command hooked her finger at her. Cynthia entered the testing room with as much confidence as she could manage. The sooner she sat her test the quicker she could go home. The room didn't have much in it, just a table and two chairs placed opposite each other. One wall had a mirror. She guessed it was two-way and that Agatha was watching through it.

A gray-haired man in his fifties, wearing a white lab coat, was sitting in one chair. He gestured to the free seat. Cynthia sat down, noting the lingering warmth of the last Synth who'd sat on it.

'For the record, please state your name,' asked the interviewer.

She released a discreet breath. 'Cynthia Glendale.'

'And how old are you?'

'Seventeen.'

The interviewer read from a tablet. 'Do you know why you're here?'

'Yes.'

'For the record, please state the reason.'

'Because a Synth killed a human.'

The interviewer looked up at her. 'How does that make you feel?'

She answered honestly. 'Sick. I am... I love humans. All life is precious.'

'Would you kill a human if they were trying to harm you?'

'I—I don't...'

If one of the Moles were trying to kill her or Anya, would she kill them first?

The voice entered her head. '*Lie!*'

'No.'

The interviewer nodded, then tapped something on the tablet. 'What if a human were attempting to harm someone you care about?'

He picked up the tablet and showed it to Cynthia.

The Sect

Her pulse raced. It was a picture of Anya.

'No, I—I would report them to a Sol.'

The interviewer nodded. He tapped the tablet again, then showed her another photo. 'Where is this, please?'

She recognized the place. 'The Station.'

'And what goes on there?'

'It's where I receive my monthly upgrades.'

The interviewer tapped his tablet again. Cynthia tried not to glance at the two-way mirror.

He held up another photo. 'Where is this place?'

It was the park where she liked to run. 'Golden Gate Fields.'

He presented another photo. 'What does this person do for a living?'

'It's a Mole.' She determined his profession from the oil stains on the front of his overalls. 'Moles service the Sect's utilities.'

Another photo. This one showed three Moles standing over a cowering Synth.

'How does this make you feel?'

She answered honestly. 'Angry.'

The interviewer lifted a brow. 'Angry enough to intervene?'

She knew what he was trying to do, what Agatha had asked him to do. The voice in her head had told her to lie. Maybe the voice wasn't a voice at all, but her conscience protecting her.

She lifted her chin. 'No, I would call for a Sol immediately. I would not intervene.'

The interviewer placed the tablet on the table and turned to the mirror behind him. He nodded before facing Cynthia once more.

'Okay, thank you. That's all.'

Cynthia rose from the chair, unsure whether she'd passed the test.

She followed the Sol out of the room and the next person was called. Cynthia sat on the floor once more. Other Synths who hadn't been tested yet watched her, probably trying to gain a clue from her demeanor about what to expect. She bunched up her legs and looped her arms around them.

An hour and six Synths later, Agatha emerged from the room on the left. She called all the Synths together. Some who had chosen the cells were returned to the recreation room.

'Thank you for your patience,' she said. 'We have tested you all and we will be returning you to the mainland now.'

Cynthia breathed out her relief. The voice in her head remained silent. The Sols, stripped of most emotions, marched forward like the bunch of blank soldiers they were. She got to her feet and followed them back to the wharf and the train. As she did, she did a quick head count. Five fewer than had arrived were leaving. Her breath hitched at the realization. Jake Jones, the first to sit the test, was one of the five.

The voice returned to soothe her consciousness. *'Well done, Cynthia Glendale.'*

'What now?' she whispered.

The Sect

'*Now, we wait.*'

19

Anya

Someone shook her awake. Anya grunted and squinted into the blackness. She saw Jason's outline above her. As her eyes adjusted, so too did his form. He had one finger on his lips.

At least he hadn't ditched her, or changed his mind. Her idea to explore alone had been a bad one. The plan relied too much on his lock picking experience.

She got up slowly, carefully, so as not to create a squeak in the cot. Next to her, Evan was snoring; Grace was on her side facing in the opposite direction.

Jason squeezed past the privacy divider. She followed him as he crept across the open-plan accommodation area to the exit door.

He stopped at the door, got out two slim pieces of metal, then started on the manual lock. Neither of them said anything while he worked. Something clicked inside the lock; Jason tried the handle.

Slowly, gently, he eased the door open, stuck his head out part way, then waved Anya on.

She glanced back one last time, then stepped into a narrow corridor, several closed doors along its length. The area was quiet. There were no cameras on the walls that she could see. Anya guessed the Sols were keeping watch, just not here.

'I guess a locked door is enough to keep us under control,' she whispered.

Jason didn't reply. Instead, he crept along the corridor and pressed his ear to each door.

He tried each handle gently. One opened for him and he checked inside.

'Hurry,' he said, pulling Anya inside what appeared to be someone's office.

It had a desk with nothing on it except for an old, chunky computer with a cream-colored keyboard. There was also a chair and an old filing cabinet that had been used to keep paper files in once, before technology put everything online. It was like being back at the museum in Sacramento, over 150 kilometers away, before it also became a Sect. It was far too dangerous to travel between Sects now, due to the danger posed by the Exiles living in the land between.

Anya looked around. 'It's so antiquated.'

'Filing cabinets can't be hacked. I heard it was the Base's backup plan for when this type of thing happens.'

'You mean they use paper records?'

'Sort of. More like a return to a decentralized

system that can't be infiltrated.' Jason turned round and faced Anya. 'I heard what you called that girl, Jessica, and Cynthia's so-called friends.'

Her blood ran hot with the memory. 'She deserved it.'

'She did, and I'm sorry for being a dick about Cynthia. She's been a better friend to you than any of those girls. You're lucky to have her.'

Hearing Jason admit that squeezed her heart.

Her voice softened. 'She has. I am.'

'Come on, let's search the room.' Jason headed for the desk and sat down on the chair. 'Someone could be back any minute.'

That's what worried her. 'And if we get caught?'

He shrugged. 'Then we're just a couple of curious teenagers. This is what we do—poke around. That's what we'll tell them.'

He clicked the ancient computer on and pulled the keyboard toward him.

Anya went over to the filing cabinets and pulled the first drawer out as quietly as she could. She checked inside. It was empty. She pulled the next one out and the next. There was nothing inside.

She relocated to Jason's shoulder. He was staring at a black screen with green lettering on it.

'I don't recognize this data. What does DOS command mean?' He shook his head and turned the computer off at the side. 'This is all junk. Come on. Maybe we can find out what's going on from a real human.'

The Sect

They left the office behind and crept along the smooth-walled corridor. It offered no place to hide if anyone appeared. But Anya already had a plan in her head. She'd begun working on it the second she and Jason had agreed to team up that afternoon. If anyone found them creeping about, she would burst into tears and act like the teenager she was expected to be. Tears had gotten her out of homework with difficult teachers, on occasion. They had also gotten her out of some housework. But only with Evan. Grace was a little more clued in to her antics.

The corridor ended at a set of double doors. Jason pushed one side open a little, then whispered, 'It's the vehicle bay. I don't see anyone around. Come on.'

He disappeared through the doors. Shaking with fear she followed him, hoping she wouldn't have to put her waterworks plan into action. The lights were off in the bay, which made it easier to creep around. Jason ducked and moved to the side of one black vehicle on the right with its nose pointed at the wall. There was a set of tall shelves on the opposite wall.

Anya smashed her back against the door of the first vehicle. 'Where is everybody?'

'I don't know.' Jason lifted his head and frowned. 'Wait, I can hear someone outside. Come on.'

He darted to the next vehicle parked in the same way as the first, then continued along the next one again until he'd reached the outer door. It had only been partially closed. Anya stayed on his heels, hearing distinct crackle from walkie talkies through the open gap in the massive doors.

Jason held a finger up to his lips. From their current position, she could barely make out what they were saying. But perhaps the opposite side might offer better acoustics. She pointed to the vehicle on the other side of the exit door. Jason nodded and ran for it. She was about to follow him when the doors opened and three Sols walked into the parking bay.

'Say that again?' said one Sol into the device.

'*I said Agatha has finished her interrogation of the Synths,*' the crackled reply came.

'What's the next step?'

'*I don't know. There's no word coming from the island...*' A pause followed. '*Wait, there's something happening there.*'

Anya cowered behind the nearest vehicle. She assumed the call was coming from someone positioned at height and who had a clear view of the island.

'*The Synths, they're boarding the train.*'

Her heart kicked into a higher gear.

'What? Why didn't anyone tell us?'

The Sol sounded rattled.

A new voice came over the walkie talkie. '*All Sols to the dock. The train's arrival is imminent...*'

The vehicle Anya was hiding behind emitted a blue light from around the door frame of the car. She heard it whir into life. With a sharp breath, she scrabbled to get to the next vehicle, before the Sol who had activated it spotted her. Her waterworks plan would have to wait.

She heard little over the thumping in her ears, barely peeking around the edge of an idle vehicle as she watched the Sols pile into the active one. It reversed, then drove out through the exit doors. Anya released a hard breath, but quickly sucked in a new one when more Sols jogged in. She squeezed out from her hiding place and raced to the end of the room. There, she flattened herself against the ground, hoping the Sols wouldn't venture down this far. To her relief, they took the vehicle closest to the door, leaving alone the only one protecting her from discovery.

The second vehicle drove off. Anya waited a moment, nose to concrete. When no more Sols appeared, she got to her feet. Two cars from the side where Jason was hiding had also been taken. She raced to the other side, worried he was clinging to the back of one.

'Jason,' she whispered.

'Yeah.' His light-brown head popped up. 'That was close.'

It was, but also the most exciting thing to have happened to her recently.

'Did you hear what the spotter said?' she asked him.

'Yeah, a train is returning to the mainland.'

'We have to check. I have to know if Cynthia is on board.'

She peeked out past one of the exit doors into the yard and studied the high, chain-link fence surrounding it. The way out appeared to be locked. She looked up at the floodlights that lit up the outside area.

'No chance in hell you're getting near that gate if the Sol watching the island is above us,' warned Jason.

That's what she thought too. She turned and checked what else was in the room. Her gaze settled on the shelves on the opposite wall.

'Maybe there's something over there,' she said, jogging over to them.

Each one had metal baskets on them holding an assortment of items. She rummaged through them. Nothing looked familiar to her. Jason helped her to look.

'Can you find something we can use?' she asked.

He nodded, and a few moments later pulled out what looked to be two pairs of binoculars.

He tossed a pair to her. 'Old fashioned, but they'll work.'

They returned to the exit and Anya looked through her binoculars. She saw Pier 45 in the distance and the train crossing the ice-cold waters. It was on the move.

It pulled up to Pier 45 and three dozen Sols—far more than had been here moments ago—rallied around the train. She couldn't see much with their giant heads in the way. The first of the passengers got off. She didn't recognize any of them. Were they the Synths? She searched the sea of heads for a blonde one.

One head matching Cynthia's hair color caught her attention. Whoever it was they were surrounded by Sols. The head bobbed through a thick cluster of Sols and to a waiting truck. The crowd parted and Anya caught a glimpse of the person's face. Cynthia! She was looking around, searching, almost memorizing her surroundings: the Sols, the vehicle, the route out.

Anya sighed with relief. 'She's there.'

'I see her,' said Jason. 'The vehicles are leaving. We need to get back to the dorm.'

'But I want to see where they're taking her.'

Jason snatched her binoculars from her. 'No time. If they're coming here, this place is going to be swarming with Sols.'

He raced back to the shelves and put the binoculars back.

When the lights of the vehicles turned on the parking bay, she stepped back in fright. Jason had already reached the inner door and was holding it open for her. She wasted no more time getting back to the corridor. Jason reached the door to the accommodation area and opened it slowly. She wished he'd hurry up.

Jason closed the door with a soft click and reworked it with his picks, to enable the locking mechanism again.

Anya backed up, sweaty and shaking with adrenaline. It looked like everyone was still asleep. She padded across the floor and slid behind the privacy divider. Jason had just made it back when she heard the inner door open. She peeked out to see several Sols step inside.

Her father stirred. 'What's going on?'

She hoped he wouldn't notice how sweaty or out

of breath she was. 'The Sols are here.'

Evan pulled back the privacy divider. Several Sols lined the entrance to the room. One by one, the Synths she'd seen from the train filed in. Her hope lifted.

A familiar face entered the room. Cynthia's parents raced over to her, hugging her long and hard.

Anya smiled at Jason, who responded with a nod.

Cynthia looked up and over, searching. When Anya stepped out of her allocated space, a wide smile spread across Cynthia's face. They stood there several beds apart, but Anya didn't care if they never hugged again. All that mattered was Cynthia was safe.

20

Cynthia

Cynthia's head throbbed with the extra voice telling her what to do. Whatever she had said in the interrogation —interview or whatever—had obviously been enough to pass Agatha's test. Five Synths fewer had left the island than had arrived. Where were they now? Was it that easy to be terminated by the Corp? She wished the voice in her head could help with that information.

Inside the warehouse filled with haphazard dividers and curious onlookers, hundreds of human gazes fixed on her and the other Synths, as they reunited with their families. Not all parents had had their loved ones return. She noticed fear on two sets of faces as they questioned where their adopted children were.

'Probably doing something important for the commander,' one replied.

But Cynthia knew better.

She saw Jessica glaring at her, arms folded,

surrounded by her pack of minions. But considering what she'd just been through, she cared little for the drama that girl created.

Her mother continued to stare at her, mouth open in disbelief, as if she were a mirage. Her bloodshot eyes told Cynthia she'd been crying. As if the well-worn tissue she clutched wasn't enough of a clue. Her father wore a stoic expression, one hand resting on her mother's back in support.

Her mother held Cynthia's face and checked her over again. 'You're sure you're okay?'

Cynthia nodded. 'I'm okay.'

'What did they do to you?'

'Nothing. They asked me some questions, that's all. It was just a precaution.'

The voice in her head whispered, *'Bide your time.'*

Other whispers reached her from the kids who went to her school. Nasty things about termination and deserving it, and 'I'm surprised to see them here.' She glared at each of them in turn, hoping they might remember why they'd been brought here. The whispers stopped. None of the parents bar one scolded their children. Prejudice had to start somewhere. Most likely it was at home.

Her mother smiled, new tears in her eyes. 'You're safe now, that's all that matters.'

Yeah, that was all that mattered. Until another Synth defied their basic programming and she was whisked off to Alcatraz again for more tests, more interrogation. More guilty-until-proven-innocent treatment.

In that moment she needed only one person. Her gaze went to Anya, still three beds apart, standing by a privacy divider, her hand gripping one arm. Her brows were pulled forward with worry. Cynthia caught a glistening on her skin, like she'd been sweating.

Damn, it was good to see her.

'Anya,' Cynthia said, closing the gap between them. She hugged her hard, loving the smell of apricot in her hair. Her shampoo. But then a pungent smell of sweat hit her. She pulled out of the embrace. 'Have you been running?'

Anya blushed. 'No! I... was worried about you. I sweat when I'm worried.' Her frown deepened. 'What the hell happened over there?'

'Nothing much. A few cognitive tests, then boom, we were being put back on the train.'

Anya pulled Cynthia away to a quieter section of the warehouse, away from the commotion of Synths reuniting with their parents. 'What kind of tests?'

She thought about telling her about the voice in her head and what it had said, how it had told her to lie during Agatha's interrogation. But it would only invite more questions Cynthia couldn't answer. The most likely explanation was that it was a glitch from her upgrade. The fact that five Synths hadn't returned to the mainland bothered her more. Any hint that her cognitive functionality might be on the fritz could make her number six.

'Nothing to worry about.' She forced a smile. 'Simple ones. What's your name, who are your parents... that sort of thing.'

The hard frown between Anya's eyes softened. She sighed. 'Why do you think the Synth killed that human earlier?'

'I have no idea. Agatha said it might have been a bad sector in his empathy functionality,' she lied.

She wasn't even sure the Techs at the Base knew why. Perhaps it had something to do with the voice in her head.

Anya eyed her, as if she didn't believe her answer. The one downside of having a best friend. They could read you better than anyone else.

'Could it have had anything to do with the upgrade?' Anya suggested. She reached out and touched Cynthia's arm. 'How do you feel?'

Cynthia stiffened beneath her gesture, then forced another smile for her astute friend. 'I feel fine. Better than fine, actually. I'm sure it's something else, something that has nothing to do with the upgrade. None of us failed the empathy tests.' Except for five Synths. 'I'm sure that's the end of the drama.'

She looked around properly for the first time. The voice in her head had distracted her enough that she hadn't questioned why a section of the human population had been gathered in one place.

'Why are you all here, in this room?' She looked at her friend. 'Was there another power outage in the Sect?'

Anya's eyes widened. 'No, I thought they would have told you. They couldn't account for all the FLC Synths, so they locked us up here and in similar holding facilities throughout Zone One. Too keep us safe, they said.'

The thought made Cynthia shudder. She hid it behind a shrug. 'Well, maybe they'll let you return home tomorrow.'

Collecting the humans from their homes and bringing them here seemed like an overreaction. Nothing like this had ever happened before, plus it was only one Synth who had killed the human. The Corp had never shown mistrust in the Synths before. In fact, it was their recommendation that Synths be integrated into society as full members. Surely they wouldn't do that if they didn't have faith in the Techs controlling the upgrades?

A yawn hit Cynthia. Spending most of the day at Alcatraz had drained her emotionally.

Anya's eyes widened. 'Oh, my God, you must be exhausted. I should let you get some sleep.'

'That would be good.' Cynthia smiled. 'Talk in the morning?'

Anya nodded. 'Yeah. Night, Super Synth.'

'Night, Mighty Mortal.'

Cynthia returned to her parents, who were waiting next to a privacy curtain on the back wall. She slipped behind it. There were three cots. She sat down on one.

'Good to have you back, love,' her mother said.

Her father nodded and smiled.

'Good to be back,' she said.

It really was.

Cynthia closed her eyes and concentrated on the soft sounds inside the large warehouse facility. The chatter had turned to whispers. It was early morning and she was sure the Synths' arrival had woken several people up.

The voice in her head was also just a whisper.

'*Bide your time,*' it repeated, softer now, like someone was walking away.

Bide her time for what?

A new tingle began inside her head and traveled down to her hands and feet. She flexed the sensation away. Then it started again, except this time it jerked her leg out to the left. She kicked her mother by accident.

Her mother stared at her. 'What was that for?'

'Sorry, m-my leg cramped.'

'Go to sleep, love. We all need it.'

Cynthia turned onto her back. What the hell had just happened? A leg cramp? She'd never had one before.

She waited for the next sensation to hit, for whatever glitch the upgrade had introduced to her system to jerk a different limb, but nothing happened.

'*Go to the vehicle bay*,' the voice whispered in her head. '*At dawn.*'

Okay, now she was irritated. She'd had enough of this extra voice telling her what to do. But fighting it was getting her nowhere.

Cynthia took a different tack.

'What should I do there?' she whispered into the dark.

The voice replied, '*You'll know.*'

21

Quintus

Creating a second power surge had been easier than Quintus had expected. Mostly because he'd disguised it as a glitch in the maintenance program. And getting access to the second room that held the code to the Synths had been easier again. All he'd had to do was wait for Shawn to come on the dawn shift. Then he'd bombarded him with a dozen questions, so Shawn had forgotten to check the firewall that was usually disabled during a surge. Except according to the logs, there had been no surge.

Quintus had then dared him to drink a liter of water. The idiot had taken him up on the bet, and an hour later had rushed off to the bathroom.

Masking the latest power surge as a glitch had been easy, but the firewall would only stay down for a short time—with or without Tech intervention. Carrying out a trial run for his final plan yesterday morning, Quintus had timed Shawn the week before, during a similar bathroom break. The guy had spent between one and three minutes there.

During the first power surge, he'd managed to tack on a new command to the last upgrade. The original had added a new voice trigger that would override the basic command functions. His extra command had given him access to one Synth's thoughts. And during yesterday morning's outage, while Shawn had been in the bathroom, Quintus had entered the second room again and slipped a kill code into the upgrade of one random ID, the one who'd gone berserk and killed the human. He'd also inserted a conflicting command into the ID numbers of five random Synths that would lower their empathetic responses. He presumed Agatha and her Sols would be too busy flapping about the murder to notice the changes. He also hoped the five defective Synths would be enough to convince the Corp that they'd found and solved their problem.

Finally, Quintus copied the data from the Synths' communications to his read-write console. One random ID number—a female—was the only one whose thoughts were visible to him. He'd been speaking to her on and off all day.

Presently, he was stuck doing extra work for Shawn in the hour before dawn. A bet was a bet and the Tech *had* drunk the water. A little extra file scrubbing was worth it for the chance to gain freedom from this hell.

What worried him now was he hadn't heard the

female Synth speak in three hours. It had surprised him how easy it had been to control her. All he'd had to do was keep his emotions in check. In control. Sound like someone worth listening to.

Shawn's voice boomed over the communications. 'You there?'

Quintus looked up at the ceiling. 'Where else would I be?'

'I'm gonna need your help today. Agatha's on my backside over getting the fileshare permissions ready. She's presenting to the Corp, but I haven't had a chance to do it.'

Fileshare. The Corp's latest demand from the Base, to enable them to see everything that went on here—day or night. Another reason to escape.

'Can you get started on it, like, now?'

It wasn't like Quintus had anything else important to do, no female Synth to whisper to.

'Sure.'

'Thanks, buddy.'

'A promise is a promise.'

Shawn clicked off, leaving Quintus to worry about the next stage of his escape plan: how to get the Synth inside the Base. An idea occurred to him and he clicked his fingers.

The vehicles, of course. They would be returning the Sols to the Base at dawn. He would order the Synth to hide beneath one. His last message to her was to go to the vehicle bay. His original plan had been for her to climb the chain-link fence and escape, but chances were high that she'd be spotted. No, this was a much better idea.

Now, he just needed a moment alone to add another message to the Synth's thoughts.

Shawn came through the line again. 'Sorry, man, but Agatha wants to see you.'

'Now?'

He'd thought she was still on Alcatraz going through the data. That's where Shawn had told him she was a few hours ago.

'Yeah.'

He tried out his new calm persona. 'Of course.'

'I'll patch you through.'

His white prison fizzled away and the cream-colored walls of Agatha's office replaced it.

She stood to the left of the desk. Her back was turned away and she was staring at a poster of New San Francisco. It was the name of this city before it became the Sect, before the Corp standardized the regions in United America closest to the coast.

'You summoned me?' he announced himself.

His voice was unusually high. A quick glance at his reflection confirmed his avatar was female.

Agatha didn't turn around. She just kept staring at the poster.

'Is there something I can help you with?' he added formally.

He really needed to send another message to his Synth.

Agatha dropped her chin to her chest and let out a

sigh. 'I'm trying to figure out what happened to this city. How did we become so easily manipulated?'

Quintus feigned innocence. 'Can't say I've noticed any manipulation.'

Except maybe for Shawn, and the Synths whose code he'd messed with.

Agatha turned slowly, her gaze on the floor. She perched on the edge of her desk. 'I've just spent most of the day on Alcatraz, watching Synths be interviewed.'

'Oh?' He feigned surprise. 'Anything interesting crop up?'

She looked up at him. 'We identified five Synths with problematic empathy responses.'

'Five, really? That's a high number.'

'This is the first time in... perhaps forever that we've had a problem with any of the first-life-cycle Synths.'

Quintus held his non-existent breath. What did Agatha know? Why had she called him here this close to dawn? He worried his plan wasn't looking so cut and dry.

She continued. 'Then there was the Synth that killed the human outside the Station.'

'What? When?'

He'd injected suitable shock into his female voice. She would be expecting a little drama from him, after all.

'Yesterday morning.' She glared at him, as though she had it all worked out. But she couldn't have. Surely she wouldn't have brought him here if that were the case? 'I can't figure it out, or why someone would mess with the upgrade. I also can't help thinking that you're involved in some way.'

Quintus emitted a nervous laugh. 'Me? How could I have done anything? You've got me confined to crappy IT duties and given me access to programming I can do nothing with.'

Agatha folded her arms. 'Quintus, let's not play games here. You could have done something during the major power outage and the reboot.'

'Like what?' He splayed his hands, hoping to neutralize any guilt in his tense posture. 'I was rendered unconscious during the reboot, just like all the other systems.'

Agatha laughed once. 'Doesn't mean you didn't find a way around it.'

'To do what exactly?'

He sensed she was on a fishing expedition. Well, he wasn't about to take the bait.

Her mouth turned down as she shrugged. 'Access the Synth data, somehow?'

'And risk permanent damage to my circuitry? You know what that firewall would do to me. I may despise that you've confined me to the scrap heap, but I have no interest in going quietly.'

'That's what worries me.'

'What, that I'd commit suicide?'

'No, that you wouldn't go quietly.'

He feigned anger. 'I'm not willing to stand here and take this. I've done nothing wrong—'

'—yet.'

'At all! So if you don't have hard proof, then return me to my room, please.'

He lifted his chin and puffed out his chest, to solidify his demand.

Agatha's lips thinned. With a sigh, she waved her hand. The office fizzled away and his white room returned.

Quintus released a breath. She had her suspicions, but she couldn't prove it. Exactly how he'd planned it.

Shawn's voice boomed overhead. 'You in trouble, man?'

'Nah, nothing I can't handle.'

'Good to hear. Don't forget about the fileshare.' How could he? 'After, I've got a long list of things for you to do.'

'Yeah.'

Story of his system-based life.

He wandered over to the wall with the code streaming down it. An additional file sat there, hidden by the other code, only visible to him under his maintenance ID. In it were the Synth's thoughts and his responses to her. But nobody ever looked closely at his maintenance logs. Or at least, he hoped they never would.

Quintus got to work for Shawn. The quicker he looked like he was working, the faster he could talk to the Synth again.

22

Anya

Anya woke a few hours later feeling restless. Cynthia and the other Synths had arrived in the accommodation warehouse in the early hours, safe and sound. She should be happy, not stressed, but something she couldn't explain bothered her.

She sat up on her cot and looked over at her family, finding their beds were empty. Maybe it was later than she thought. With no natural light in the warehouse, day and night appeared to be the same.

She pushed the itchy blanket off her and got up. A murmur of noise on the other side of the privacy divider reached her. She heard her mother whispering to someone.

'She's not with Anya,' Grace said.

Anya's heartbeat crashed against her ribs again. She squeezed past the privacy screen to see her family huddled around Cynthia's parents. Her stomach somersaulted.

Others were still sleeping, but some were awake and talking softly. She hurried over to her parents.

'What's going on?' she said in a low whisper.

Her father turned, a worried look on his face. 'Love, Cynthia's gone.'

Anya's gaze darted between her parents. 'What do you mean gone?'

'Her parents woke up to find her neither in her cot nor anywhere else in this warehouse.'

Anya did a visual check of the room. She knew her best friend better than anyone. If anyone could figure out her whereabouts, it would be her. It was a large enough space. Cynthia could simply be hiding.

'Have you checked the entire room?'

'We have,' said Grace. She gripped Anya's arm. Too tight. 'Did she say anything to you last night?'

Anya frowned as she tried to recall, then shook her head. 'Nothing.'

Cynthia's mother addressed Evan. 'Where would she have gone?'

Grace released Anya and answered her. 'She's fine, Gloria. I'm sure of it.'

Anya left the adults to their speculation. She wandered away from them, dazed by this news. She stared at the door she and Jason had snuck out of last night. A hand on her shoulder startled her. She spun round, surprised and disappointed to see Jason standing there. She'd been hoping for Cynthia.

'Don't do that!'

She didn't mean to snap, but his timing was

lousy.

'Sorry.' Jason withdrew his hand and stuffed it into his pocket. 'Are you sure Cynthia didn't say anything to you last night? I was thinking about it after the Synths piled in. We have no idea what the Corp ordered to have done to them on Alcatraz.'

Anya tried to think back to what they'd talked about. If it would help locate her she would try.

'I asked her why she thought the Synth killed that human. She replied that it might have had something to do with a damaged sector in his empathy functionality.' She frowned at her brother. 'Does that even make sense?'

Jason shrugged. 'It's possible.'

'But isn't empathy checked during the upgrades, to make sure no bad sectors have formed?'

'Maybe. Anything else?'

'Uh, I asked her how she felt. She said fine, but there was something off about her.'

Jason sighed, keeping one eye on the room. 'Something's going on here, and I'm worried it's more than one Synth gone crazy.'

'Like what?'

'I don't know, but I think we need to find Cynthia.'

'How? We're stuck in here.'

'With the Synths cleared, we'll be allowed to return home. Or at least that's what Dad said.'

Anya hugged herself. She hoped that were true, and that this really was the end of it. She and Cynthia had been through so much. But Jason's concerns bothered her.

'Where might she have gone, Anya?'

She met Jason's gaze. 'I don't know.'

Maybe she didn't know Cynthia as well as she thought.

Jason nodded at their parents, still talking to Cynthia's. 'Then I think we should involve Dad. He might be able to help.'

'What, no!' Her squeaky voice drew a few curious glances. She lowered the tone. 'What if he tells the commander of the Base?'

'Agatha?' Jason shrugged. 'Would that be such a bad idea? Maybe she can help.'

Or maybe she would order Cynthia's termination.

There could only be one plan. 'We need to find Cynthia first. She might not be thinking straight, or she might be fine. But the instant we start blabbing about her strange behavior, we could end up making things worse for her.'

Jason folded his arms. 'So what do you suggest?'

'We keep this between us until we can locate her.'

'And if she's been compromised?'

'You just suggested we tell that Agatha woman. Her Sols were over on the island with the Synths. We saw her return. What if she was the one who did something to Cynthia?'

Jason uncrossed his arms and sighed again. 'Okay, let's do it your way. We don't tell anyone else about this.'

She extended her hand, looking for something more concrete from him. Jason shook it. 'Deal.'

$$\Omega$$

An hour later, the accommodation area was flooded with Sols. One ordered the residents to collect their things and line up by the door.

'The danger has been dealt with,' he said. 'You are free to return to your homes.'

'About time,' muttered Grace. 'I've had enough of peeing in a communal bathroom.'

So had Anya. It would be good to see home again, but her mind was stuck on Cynthia's whereabouts. Where could she have gone? Golden Gate Fields, perhaps?

She gripped her backpack tight and waited near the exit with her family. A Sol stood nearby, thick armed and broad shouldered. His eyes flashed with a look that matched the hardness of his black body armor.

She must have been staring because the Sol slid his ice-cold gaze to Anya. She flicked her gaze forward, pulse throbbing in her ears.

Ahead, the residents followed the person in charge. Anya shuffled along when her turn allowed, moving until her family had reached the bright outside. Barely dawn by her reckoning. The Sol vehicles were moving out. The buses that had brought them to the warehouse lined up once more. Anya waited her turn to board a bus.

The bus took off and the streets whizzed by, looking eerily abandoned in the early morning light. Not a soul was out. A day lost for everyone. Soon, life would return to normal in the Sect. She hoped.

Their stop arrived and Anya jumped up, needing out, feeling claustrophobic in this confined space. Her feet hit the pavement hard and she slipped down the alley to their front door.

'Home sweet home,' Grace announced with glee when her father opened the door.

Anya raced upstairs to her bedroom and dropped her backpack on the bed. Finally out of the tech-blocked warehouse and off the bus, where there'd been no privacy, she tried her comms. The display on her hand fired up.

'*Yes!*'

Anya dialed Cynthia's number. Unlike the day before, the call now maintained a connection, but her friend didn't pick up.

'Where are you, Cynthia?' Anya muttered.

Someone knocked on her door. She closed the connection. 'Yeah?'

Jason appeared. 'Anything?'

'No. I don't know where she might have gone.'

He waved for her to follow. 'I might have an idea. Come on.'

Anya hopped off the bed. Her heavy heart lightened at not having to figure this out alone. She followed Jason into his bedroom. The curtains were half open, making the room look dank and depressing. A ripe stench hit her. She pinched her nose.

'Ever hear of cracking open a window once in a while?'

Jason ignored her and pulled open the top drawer of his dresser. He took out a small screen with an antenna attached to it.

'What's that?'

Anya released her nose and sat down. She'd put up with the smell for a little mystery.

Jason joined her on the bed and showed her. 'It's a tracking device.'

It didn't look like a tracking device. Not that she'd ever seen one. But this wasn't sleek and it wasn't discreet.

'Don't you need a tracking device to be on a person?'

That was her assumption anyway.

'It's monitoring one.' Jason hit the screen a few times and brought up a map. On it, a red light blinked. 'I've been doing a side project.' He blushed a little. 'I've been using this to track Cynthia.'

She stood up, hands on hips. 'Excuse me?'

Jason set the screen on his lap. 'Hear me out.'

Anya folded her arms in defiance. *This had better be good.*

'I was hearing rumors that the Synths were causing trouble down at the station and the market.'

'You mean the Moles were. They hate Synths.'

'I know. Well, I wanted to see if I could tell a

human and Synth apart. It's not that easy, you know.'

'That's the whole point! We're supposed to be living together, not one side pitted against the other.'

Jason glared at her. 'Listen to me.'

Anya rolled her eyes. 'Fine.'

'I managed to isolate the signature that identifies her as Synth, not human.'

'Yeah, it's buried in her code. She told me about it. It's how she accesses the Station.'

'Well, the last few times she was here, I was able to get a fingerprint analysis from her.'

Anya controlled her breathing. 'You did what?'

'The code is in her fingerprint. Did you know that?'

She hadn't. But it made sense if Cynthia was using her thumb to gain access to the Station. 'So?'

He picked up the screen, showed her the blinking red dot. 'I can track her ID with this. It knows her ID now, so wherever she goes it can find it—her.'

She sat down on the bed again, feeling calmer. 'She's innocent in all this.'

'I know. And I'm sorry for treating her differently. Glen is also a Synth, and he's been a good friend to me.'

She believed him. Anya turned the screen to face her. The dot was set over the warehouse facility they'd just left. 'Says here Cynthia is still at the warehouse. That's not possible. Unless... could she be hiding there?'

Jason shook his head and hit a refresh button. 'It's

not real-time data. I can only estimate where she's been in the last hour.'

Anya watched the wheel spin on screen. Then the dot changed location.

Anya frowned. 'Why is it headed for the Base?'

'She must be on her way there.'

That didn't make sense. 'She's never been there. She's never even mentioned it, except in passing. And her code wouldn't give her access to it.'

Jason frowned at the screen. 'Why would Cynthia be on her way to the military stronghold?'

'I don't know.' Anya stood up. If anyone found Cynthia she would be in serious trouble. 'We need to get to her before Agatha and her team do.'

23

Cynthia

The voice in her head told her to get up. Cynthia's leg jerked to the side; her other leg followed suit. It felt like someone had tied strings to her limbs and was working her like a Marionette doll. But the invasion went deeper than that. Someone was working her mind, influencing the reasoning center of her brain.

Someone controlled her mind and her body was letting them.

Cynthia checked the darkened space inside the warehouse. Hearing and seeing little movement, she got up with a confidence that she would not be spotted. Her parents slept soundly beside her—exhausted and relieved by her safe return, no doubt.

She glanced over to where Anya slept, seeing nothing beyond the privacy screen around her and her family. She hated that she'd lied to Anya earlier, but what choice did she have? Without knowing what was going on, she couldn't risk bringing more people into it, or putting anyone else on Agatha's radar.

'*Grab something sharp,*' the voice commanded.

She checked around where her father had left his clothes. All Earthers carried utility knives. Her father was no exception.

She spotted his pants folded and stacked neatly next to his cot. She slipped the knife out of the holder attached to his belt.

'*Head for the exit.*'

The unseen person worked her limbs and forced Cynthia to jog to the exit. She kept her steps light and even. *That* was her doing. At the door she pressed the handle down, finding it locked. Not a surprise there.

'*Pick the lock. You know how to do it.*'

A file appeared before her, one only she could see. She had many files in her head. Most had been placed there during previous upgrades. Most were encrypted. Some remained open, containing information on the different skills she could try out when she reached her second life cycle. Like a teaser before the main event.

This file was none of those. It was new. She thought it open, as she did any file she wanted to access in her head. It contained a new set of skills that were on the unapproved list of skills for this Sect.

Thief. A skill an Exile was more likely to have. But there it was, including detailed instructions on how to pick a lock.

Cynthia opened up the utility knife and jammed the tip of it into the lock. She wiggled it. Something released and she opened the door, slowly. Peeking out, she checked for possible Sols but found the corridor to be empty. Cynthia entered the dark corridor and stole along its length, heading in a westerly direction toward the outside and where she knew the vehicles would be parked. The voice needed her to leave this place, but where she was going wasn't clear yet.

She came upon a quiet vehicle bay and exhaled softly, dumping a little of her stress. A low light filtered through the crack in the double doors leading outside.

'*Sun will be up soon. The Sols will be returning to the Base. Make sure you hitch a ride.*'

She had no idea what that meant, but an image of her clinging to the underside of the vehicle flashed in her mind.

'No way,' she protested.

It would mean termination if she got caught. But her limbs disobeyed her head and walked her inside. Something deeper compelled her to try. Perhaps her most recent upgrade had given a boost to the risk-taking part of her brain.

As if on autopilot, she lay on the floor of the vehicle bay and shimmied under the third vehicle in one row. There, she found four anchor points: two for her hands and two for her feet. Cynthia stayed like that for the next hour, clinging to the anchors, unmoving. Before long, noise reached her from the corridor outside. The lights flicked on and the vehicles gave a little shudder, passing their fear onto her. But still she held on, like a damn Sol on power drugs. Her heart pounded in her chest, her hands raw from gripping for so long, but her thoughts were crystal clear about the task ahead—a task she had not agreed to.

The sound of chatter increased in the bay.

'Agatha is releasing the residents now,' said one Sol.

'That's it? That's the end of the crisis?'

'Apparently so.'

Two sets of feet stopped inches from Cynthia's blistering hands. The doors opened and the vehicle rocked a little as the pair got in.

'*Come to me,*' said the voice in her head.

Cynthia gripped tighter, even though her sweaty hands were losing grip and reason begged her to let go.

The car reversed out of its spot and headed out into the early dawn light. The wind tore at Cynthia's limbs and face. At least it dried her sweat, making her grip more effective. The vehicle turned onto a quiet street, then began a steady climb up into the San Bruno Mountain. The voice was taking her to the Base, she realized, the only place in a position overlooking all the Sect.

After a few minutes the vehicle slowed. Cynthia could barely hold on. Her hands were stinging, her shoulders cramped. She desperately wanted to let go, but something worked her muscles, forced her to maintain a grip, to keep going for a few minutes more.

A gate opened and the vehicle drove inside. When the noise switched from a breeze to an echo, she knew the vehicle was inside the Base. She'd never been to this place. She'd never had any reason to before now.

But something—someone—wanted her to come. And she had no will to disobey the command.

The vehicle came to a stop inside a cool space. She waited for the Sols to get out and for the vehicle to turn itself off.

Holding her breath, Cynthia waited. All noise diminished to a faint echo. She released the grips and dropped to the floor with a thud. Exhausted, Cynthia rubbed the pain out of her fingers and palms, then rolled quietly out from under the vehicle.

'You're inside. Hurry. You have to get to the Control Room. That's where I am. I can show you the way, but you'll have to do the rest.'

She said nothing, terrified that any reply she made to this voice would hint she was crazy and out of control.

A file flashed up with a map. *'Follow it to the Control Room.'*

She crept along the corridor. There was no sign of life. Perhaps it was too early and the place had a skeleton crew on. All of the team were likely asleep or down at the warehouse.

She found the Control Room that the voice had led her to. It had one wall of screens and a long console with blinking lights. She was no Tech. Why was she here?

'Lock the door.'

With a click she followed the instructions

'Don't worry; you have the skills to do this.

Check your upgrade files.'

She did. One file one marked Execute had Control Room before the.exe file extension. She opened it and a file delivered a blast of information to her memory banks. She gripped the console, bracing against the assault of information, before breathing out her stress.

'Congratulations, you are a Tech. Now, get me out of here.'

She stared at the console and the information on display. Lines of code dripped down the screens. She understood it. She could read it.

'Quintus,' she breathed out.

'Yes. Can you see me now?'

'I can.'

'I need you to disable the firewall on my prison.'

She didn't understand why she was doing it, but her fingers had other plans. They glided over the touch screen, re-organizing data into different sectors.

Someone tried the door handle. She heard someone say, 'Why is this door locked?'

Cynthia concentrated on her task. She pulled chunks of code back to reveal the little room Quintus had been confined to.

'Why are you in there?'

'A misunderstanding. I need to get out before it's too late. Can you help?'

Her brain said no, but her fingers worked the console like she was one with it. Before she knew it, she'd reached the firewall rules keeping Quintus under control.

'*That's it,*' Quintus breathed. '*I can see you now. Disable it.*'

Someone jiggled something in the lock.

Cynthia poised her fingers over the console once more.

24

Anya

Getting out of the house was easier than Anya had expected. After nearly a full day spent in a warehouse with no natural light, Evan and Grace were all for her and Jason getting fresh air. But Anya suspected it was more likely her parents were sick of the sight of them. Apparently, too much time cooped up in one place demanded a little time apart after.

She and Jason took the train to Zone One and a local bus to the start of the San Bruno Mountain road. Jason had his backpack with the homemade tracking software inside. From there, it was about two kilometers up the climbing road before the entrance to the Base. The summit that had once been accessible to hikers had been subsumed by the visible part of the Base—the part that was not inside the mountain.

She looked up at the road ahead of them. The access road leading up there would take some effort to climb, and she and Jason would be seen if they stayed on it. Jason climbed a short way up and onto a rarely used trail that ran parallel to the road the Sols used.

'Are you ready?' Jason asked.

No, but this was Cynthia and Anya would make herself ready. She nodded.

'I've been trying to work out why she'd even come to a place she's never spoken about, and I've reached one conclusion.'

Jason fixed one of his straps that had gotten twisted. 'What's that?'

'Someone is making her come here.'

'What, you mean like calling her to the Base? Is that even a thing for Synths?'

'Not that I know of. Cynthia never mentioned it.'

'Or she didn't know to mention it.' He hiked the backpack up on his shoulder. 'Come on.'

They followed the old trekking path, which was hidden by overgrown trees, and followed the road to their left. It wasn't long before both of them were panting from the steep incline.

Anya tried to reason out her friend's behavior. 'Cynthia received her upgrade recently. She's never done anything like this before. But then we had two power outages in the space of a month. What if someone is controlling... the outages *and* Cynthia?'

Jason stopped and shook his head. 'You mean one of Agatha's team? What would they get out of it?'

The elevation sharpened suddenly and Anya's legs and lungs burned more. She puffed out a hard breath. Sweat tightened her pale skin.

'I wasn't thinking the influence was one of us,' she wheezed.

Jason stopped. Anya steadied her fast breaths, grateful for the break.

'You mean another Synth?' he puffed out.

She shrugged, her words broken by heavy breaths. 'I don't know how the communication works... between them, but what if... someone slipped a message... into the last upgrade and only Cynthia heard it? It would explain... her coming here.'

Jason resumed his climb. Anya followed him, less enthusiastic about doing the same. The pain in her legs returned almost instantly. She vowed to get fit after this, like Cynthia.

'I haven't thought... about it before,' Jason managed through a flurry of breaths, 'but the code... for the Synths... is stored in the Base. If someone—' he glanced back at Anya, '—or something—gained access to it... they could make... the Synths do anything.'

She stopped a moment, unable to talk and walk anymore. Jason waited for her. At least they were well hidden by the overgrown trees on the side of the hill.

She regained enough energy to reply. 'So why this? They could have ordered them... to do anything... but one Synth killed a human. That was it.'

'Was that part of what this person wanted to do?'

'I don't know. Come on, let's keep going.'

They carried on up the old hiking trail. Anya's breaths became even more labored.

'So why... only... Cynthia?' she puffed out.

'Someone or something wants... her... to do something.'

That was obvious. 'But... not... human.' Her breaths turned sharp, and so did her answers. 'No point.'

'No, someone without... form. A program, perhaps.'

Anya knew little about the Base and what went on there.

They both stopped talking. It had become impossible. All that passed between them for the rest of the climb was the sound of heavy breathing and crunchy steps.

A tall and smooth, light-gray wall cutting into the side of the mountain and rising up from below blocked their progress on the old trail.

'We have to rejoin the road now,' said Jason.

It was a risk that they might be seen by a Sol, but there was no way either of them would get over the smooth wall. They slid down the embankment to the concrete road and resumed their walk.

The steel gate allowing access inside the Base came into view, and the elevation leveled out. Just in time too. Anya's legs were about to give way.

She crumpled to the ground, back smashed against the wall, hopefully out of view of any possible cameras this high up.

Jason joined her, but remained on his feet. He took out the tracking device and checked it. 'She's still here. Inside, according to this.'

After a few extra breaths, Anya looked up at him. 'How are we getting inside?' She looked at the imposing, solid-steel gate. 'There's no way you're picking *that* lock.'

'Actually, I was hoping there might be a pedestrian gate—'

An alarm sounded close by. Its squeal cut Jason off.

Anya jumped to her feet. 'What's that?'

Jason raced over to the gate. He pulled it to the side and it moved.

'Security appears to be down.' He breathed out. 'It could be Cynthia. If we're going to do this, it has to be now.'

Anya didn't need asking twice. 'Let's go.'

Jason opened the gate enough that they could squeeze through the gap. Then he heaved it closed again. Ahead of them was the entrance inside the Base, which had been bored into the side of the mountain. They stood in the yard to the front. It contained no activity, just a few empty vehicles.

'Over there.'

Jason pointed to a door next to a larger entrance that was most likely meant for vehicles.

He ran over to it. Anya kept close, not wanting to get separated.

'What if someone catches us?' she asked.

Jason tried the handle. It clicked open. 'I wasn't planning on getting caught.'

She marveled at this brave, young man who had

been an average brother to her for sixteen years. When had he become cool?

With a shake of her head, she watched Jason open the door. He waved for her to follow. The air inside the Base was cool. The alarm shrilled even louder inside. Anya covered her ears to dull the ache.

No Sols and no Base personnel were active in the access corridor leading farther inside.

Jason checked his tracking device.

'This thing isn't accurate enough,' he shouted. 'If she's going to be anywhere it will be at a console. Come on.'

Fear paralyzed her for a moment. But then Cynthia's face flashed in her mind, and the thought moved her on.

The noise continued to shrill in a long beat, followed by a break, then two shorter beats, before it started the cycle over. It worked well to disorientate her. She kept close to Jason as he jogged along the smooth, concrete path next to a road with a similar surface.

The route they were on split into two different directions. The road carried on straight, but the path veered off to the left. They reached a door that would take them farther inside. Jason tried it. The door opened.

'Security must still be down,' he yelled over the alarm.

Her heart beat faster. What the hell was Cynthia up to?

The Sect

Jason followed the new path down a corridor, entering the new space first. Anya looked around the new area. It was more homely here, closer to a barracks with on-site accommodation than a place of work. The walls had been painted a cool blue color. The concrete floor was a nondescript gray. She thought she smelled coffee.

'Where would she be?' she shouted over the noise that was making her ears ache.

She stuck her fingers in them.

Jason didn't answer. He just tried all the rooms along the way. A uniformed Sol appeared from one room. He startled when he saw them.

'What are you doing here?' he shouted.

He released his weapon from his hip holster and pointed it at them. Jason cursed. She heard that clearly enough. He raised his hands. Anya did the same; the pain in her ears returned.

The Sol shouted 'Intruders!' into his sleeve.

Before long, more Sols arrived. A black woman brought up the rear of the team. Anya recognized her instantly.

Agatha. The commander of this Base. She'd ordered them to leave the houses and go to the accommodation. She'd ordered the tests on the Synths on Alcatraz.

'Arrest them!' Agatha yelled over the siren. 'And can someone turn that damn thing off?'

Anya lifted her hands higher. 'Wait! We can help.'

Agatha frowned as if she struggled to hear her. Then the shrill cut out and the commander let out a sigh. 'Thank God for that.' She turned her full attention to Anya and Jason. 'You are both trespassing on Corp property. That carries serious penalties.'

'We can help,' Anya repeated. 'We think there's a first-life-cycle Synth here and she's under the influence of someone or something.'

Agatha's eyes widened. 'A Synth? How?' She pointed at her team. 'Go find her.'

Most of the team dispersed, leaving Agatha with three Sols. Enough to control Anya and her brother.

'Please, she's my friend,' Anya said. 'I can talk to her.'

'What is she even doing here? First-life-cycle Synths are programmed to avoid this place. Is she responsible for my security breach?'

'We think so but, please, she's never done anything like this before.' Anya hoped the woman would see reason. 'We think she may have received a message during her last upgrade telling her to come here.'

'A message? From whom?' Agatha's eyes widened suddenly. 'Oh no. I knew I should have listened to my gut.'

She marched off. Anya went to follow but one of the Sols stopped her.

Agatha turned and waved. 'Let them through.'

Anya pushed past the young men in Sol uniforms and kept up with a fast-walking Agatha. Jason was right behind. The commander took a left turn and entered a room with a console. Two frazzled men were racing from one end of the console to the other.

'What happened here?' Agatha asked a nervous, young man.

'Came on duty to find the door locked. Then a girl came rushing out.'

'What did she do?' Agatha demanded. 'I want an update on Quintus.'

One of the men combed his fingers through his hair nervously. 'He's in his room, commander, as usual.'

Agatha pushed him aside and checked the screen. Anya checked it too and saw a white room with an individual inside it. An entity dressed in white was sitting on the floor, back turned to the viewer.

Jason neared the screen. He pointed at something. 'That's on a loop.'

Agatha stared at him. 'Excuse me?'

He pointed again. 'See there?' Anya watched the image, seeing nothing odd. Then it skipped almost imperceptibly. 'It's replay footage.'

Agatha drew back from the screen, her mouth agape. 'Leo, get in there. Find out where Quintus is.'

Leo typed a few commands. After a minute he said, 'He's masking his whereabouts.'

Agatha stepped back, clearly in shock. She covered her mouth for a moment.

Then she composed herself. 'Find him!'

'Yes, Commander.'

Anya didn't understand. 'I thought we were looking for my friend. Who's Quintus?'

'Oh, we are,' Agatha replied. 'Quintus is a sentient program that I've been keeping under control. And now your Synth has set him free.'

The commander's walkie talkie crackled, making Anya jump.

'*We found her, Commander.*'

Agatha clicked the side of the device. 'Take her to my office.' She hooked a finger at Anya and Jason. 'You two, come with me. You're going to help me get to the bottom of this mess.'

25

Anya

Anya and Jason followed Agatha into a large, tall area with rough, stone walls and a smooth, concrete floor. Several vehicles similar to the ones parked at the warehouse were next to a set of metal stairs. They led up to an elevated floor and a prefab. Agatha climbed the stairs, her shoes clacking noisily against the metal. Anya kept close as the commander opened the door to the prefab and walked inside.

Anya peered into what she presumed was Agatha's office. Waiting there were two Sols, standing either side of a seated Cynthia.

Her friend had her head buried in her hands. Her shoulders shook.

Anya burst into the room, ignoring the hard stares the Sols were giving her. 'Cynthia!'

Her friend looked up in shock. Her eyes were red raw. Synths were programmed with emotions and knew right from wrong. They felt everything the Corp meant them to feel.

Anya dropped to her knees in front of her. 'Are you okay?'

A worried-looking Cynthia flicked her nervous gaze to Agatha then to Anya. 'What are you doing here?' She looked past her. 'And Jason? I don't understand.'

Anya gripped one of her hands. 'We came looking for you. Agatha found us first.'

Cynthia pulled her hand out of Anya's and buried her face again. With a sigh, Anya got to her feet.

She turned to Agatha. 'What's going to happen to her?'

'I'm not sure yet.' The commander of the Base paced in front of her desk. She stopped suddenly and said to the Sols, 'Leave us, please.'

The Sols glanced at each other. 'But Commander, the Synth...'

Agatha waved away their concern. 'It's fine. I need to speak to her alone.'

The Sol pair left. The instant they did, the mood in the room lightened. Even Cynthia sat up with more confidence.

'What have I done?' she whispered to Agatha.

The commander replied coldly, 'You've released a dangerous sentient into our systems, that's what you've done.'

Cynthia's lower lip wobbled. 'I didn't know what I was doing. He... he was just a voice inside my head. He gave me new skills that allowed me to pick locks, and strength to hold onto the underside of a Sol vehicle.'

With a shake of her head, Agatha perched on the edge of her desk. 'So that's how you got inside!'

Anya waited with a quiet Jason. She turned to him. 'What do we do?'

Her brother, who usually had all the answers, just shrugged. 'I'm not a Tech. It's not my area of expertise.'

Cynthia looked up at the pair and smiled weakly. 'Thanks for caring enough to follow me. I'm sorry if you're in trouble.'

Anya looked at Agatha. 'We're not in trouble, right, Agatha?'

The Base commander appeared to be deep in thought.

She looked up, distracted. 'What?'

'When can Cynthia leave?'

Her and Jason's safety didn't matter right now. What mattered was fixing this for Cynthia.

The commander became agitated, pointing at each of them. 'Oh, no. None of you leaves until this matter is resolved. You hear me?'

She and Jason were no Techs. Anya didn't see how they could help. But if they could free Cynthia...

'What can we do? Name it. We're here to help.'

The woman sighed. 'I'm not sure. Quintus isn't someone who can be reasoned with. I had him under control and now he's God knows where. He's dangerous. If he can reprogram a Synth to come here and take over, he can do much worse with more freedom.'

Hadn't Cynthia said she'd received new skills during the upgrade?

She looked at her friend, who was wide-eyed like a scared deer. 'How did you release Quintus?'

Cynthia frowned. 'I... I knew what to do. He gave me the skill to do it.'

'So, Cynthia knows Tech,' said Anya. 'Can't we use her skills in some way?'

Agatha shook her head. 'I don't want her near my systems. Quintus helped us to build the Synths. He's used her once. He knows how to use her again.'

'Where is he now?'

'Out of his read-write prison, that's all I know.' Agatha rubbed her forehead. 'My Techs are searching for him as we speak.'

'So,' said Jason. 'If the issue is that Quintus knows the Synths well enough to manipulate them, why don't you strip him of his memories? Make him forget how to build them.'

Anya liked that idea. 'Let's do that.'

But Agatha shook her head. 'Quintus is clever. He knows how to get around and knows how our systems work. He's not going to allow me to capture him long enough to do that.'

Jason began to pace the room. The wannabe Neer loved problem solving. Anya not so much. She preferred to take life as it came to her. But recent events had her wishing she'd been more prepared for this.

A call came through Agatha's walkie talkie. She answered it. 'Yes.'

'Commander, it's Leo.'

Agatha visibly clenched. 'Where is he?'

'He's in the primary systems, but he's hit a block and he can't get out.'

Anya wondered where "out" was for him. Surely the primary systems were the end of the line?

'Out?' she asked Agatha.

'Out of the Base controls and into the Sect,' the commander said. 'Households, public spaces, anywhere technology is.'

She clicked a button on the side of her old radio. Anya assumed the use of the old-style radio was to ensure Quintus couldn't hijack it.

'Keep him there,' Agatha ordered.

'We'll try, but he's going to figure out how to get out.'

'Then we'll come up with a solution. You and Shawn do what you can to contain him. Out.'

Agatha clicked the button and placed the radio down on her desk.

Behind Anya, Jason muttered to himself, as he often did when working on a Neer problem at home.

He stopped muttering and said, 'What does this Quintus character want? What's his motivation?'

'To be free, I suppose.' Agatha eyed Cynthia. 'Did he say anything to you?'

Cynthia looked up with rounded, bloodshot eyes. 'He wanted me to free him, but not out here, in the system.'

Jason snapped his fingers. 'Hansel and Gretel.'

'Excuse me?' said Agatha.

'The fairy tale. Hear me out. The children were lured to the house made of candy. Why don't we offer Quintus what he wants most: his freedom?'

'Because he's a dangerous entity and can't be trusted.'

'No, I don't mean we set him free,' he said. 'You offer him power, make him think he's in control, but really he'll be trapped.'

Anya glanced back at Jason. 'That idea's not half bad.' He stuck his tongue out at her. She flashed a smile and faced Agatha. 'Is there anywhere like that we can put him?'

Anywhere that would mean Cynthia could leave.

Agatha straightened up. She walked to the other side of her monitor and swiped at it several times. A 3D hologram of a concentrically designed city appeared in the air before her.

'This is one of our military testing bases,' she said.

Anya squinted at the orderly looking city with a tall, white building at the center. She'd never seen it before. 'Where *is* this?'

'It's part of a vast plot of land the other side of the Base. It's not officially part of the Sect. It's a place the Corp has allocated us to train the Sols, to test out new agricultural ideas. It's used for the overflow of manufacturing.'

A training base? A testing site? The Corp was starting to reveal its secrets. But she still had one problem with the idea.

She pointed at the mystery city. 'How would that place trap Quintus when this one can't?'

Jason made a suggestion. 'If this other place has power, promise it to Quintus. What does he know about the place?'

Agatha frowned. 'Nothing. It's not on the map. It's not part of the Sect. We run it off a separate network.'

The commander's eyes widened as if an idea had hit her. She picked up the walkie talkie. 'Leo?'

'We're still monitoring him, Commander. He hasn't moved but he's searching for a way out.'

'No, I want you to call all Techs in. We have an idea.'

'We?'

'Hurry.'

'Yes, Commander.'

Agatha clicked off and walked over to where a quiet Cynthia sat. She hunkered down to her level. 'I have an idea. Will you help?'

Cynthia nodded softly. 'Anything.'

Anya didn't like her making such wild promises. She gripped her friend's shoulder. 'Within reason, Agatha. What's your idea first?'

Agatha stood up. 'If we can trap Quintus in our spare military base, then we can perform a mind wipe on him. That would neutralize the entity. But getting him there is the tricky part. We may need to give him what he wants.'

'Freedom?' Anya shook her head. 'I don't understand.'

But Jason's tight shoulders said he did. 'You want to let Quintus use Cynthia's body to cross, don't you?'

Before Anya could protest, Cynthia said, 'I'll do it.'

She rounded on her friend. 'The hell you will.'

Would nobody think about this for a damn moment?

'How long would Quintus have control of her?' she asked Agatha.

'Long enough to get him inside the city. We would block his connection to this place, giving Cynthia enough time to upload him to the system there.'

'And what happens to Cynthia?'

Agatha twisted her hands together. 'Assuming Quintus doesn't ruin it, she should come out of it unharmed.'

'Should?' Anya laughed. 'Unless you can guarantee her safety, she's not doing anything for you.'

'I'm afraid that's not up to you,' said the commander. 'Cynthia is the reason we're having this conversation.'

Anya knew it, but she still had to try to keep her friend safe.

Cynthia surprised her by touching her arm. 'Anya, it's okay.'

The Sect

She was no longer seated.

Anya tried to calm her breathing. 'I don't want you to do this if you're not safe.'

All she could see was her best friend in danger.

'I caused this—I need to fix it.'

'But it wasn't your fault. You were unlucky that Quintus picked you.'

Cynthia smiled, and Anya knew her friend's mind was made up. 'I think I know what I want to be when I move into my second life cycle. A Tech.'

A hardened lump formed in the back of Anya's throat. She flung her arms around her best friend and buried her face in her blonde hair. 'I love you, Super Synth.'

'I love you too, Mighty Mortal.'

Anya pulled back, wiping a tear away. Her resolve hardened with the action.

Lifting her chin, she glared at Agatha. 'You'd better make sure she's okay.'

The commander nodded. 'I'll do everything in my power to bring her back to you safely.'

26

Cynthia

Cynthia shook with fear as she stood next to Anya, Jason and Agatha in the Control Room, the same one she'd just been in when she'd allowed Quintus to control her. *Stupid, stupid!*

Shawn and Leo joined their huddle while other Techs worked the console.

'How will this work?' asked Anya.

Cynthia didn't care. She was doing this, no matter how dangerous it was.

Agatha nodded to one of the Techs in the huddle. 'Leo?'

The young man cleared his throat. 'We need to set up a trap for Quintus.'

She didn't see how that would work. Quintus hadn't been controlling her for long but she sensed that he'd known exactly how Cynthia's mind worked, what she'd been thinking.

'He's not going to fall for that,' she said softly.

'No,' said Leo, 'but you need to offer him something he can't get where he is.'

More time spent with Quintus? Her organic heart bashed against her ribs, making it hard to breathe.

Anya grabbed her hand, squeezed it. 'You don't have to do this. You can say no.'

'But we'd rather you didn't,' added Agatha. 'This might be our only way to secure Quintus and ensure the future safety of all Synths.'

Cynthia looked up at the commander, dressed in a bright-green pants suit, black hair pulled back tight from her dark face, brown eyes alert, focused. She didn't see that she had much choice. And she definitely couldn't walk away from it, not if it meant protecting other innocent Synths from similar attacks.

'And if I don't do this?'

She needed all the facts. She had to know what would happen if she didn't help and Quintus escaped the Base.

'The worst case scenario?' said Agatha. Cynthia nodded. 'All the first-life-cycle Synths would be terminated, effective immediately. The Corp would insist upon it. If Quintus was able to command one Synth to kill a human, imagine what he might do if he got control of the Station? We'd have no choice but to wipe the entire program and start over.' She sighed. 'Chances are high the Corp wouldn't want us starting again. They would most likely see the Synths as a portal to future attacks.'

Cynthia's mouth went dry. 'You mean take them

offline permanently?'

Agatha nodded.

'Can't you just turn Quintus off? Delete him from the system?' asked Jason.

He'd never said so much as a hello to her any time she'd visited Anya. Cynthia was still trying to figure out what he was doing here.

Agatha shook her head. 'Quintus knows everything about us. He can only be contained at this stage. If he got wind we were trying to delete his program, he would likely slip code into the system, resurrect himself later.'

Next to Cynthia Anya huffed. 'If you knew him to be that dangerous, why did you let it get this far?'

'It's a long story. But in a nutshell, Quintus was one of the original designers of the Synths' base code. That was a major failing on the part of the Corp. Quintus has full knowledge of their systems, systems that we can't access right now. He has maneuvered himself into a position of power.'

Cynthia had heard enough. The time for talking was over. 'What do I need to do? I don't care what it is. We need to stop him.'

Leo said, 'We need to set up a trap for him, make him think he's lost control here and he has no other way out.'

'And I should just contact him now?' She hadn't heard his voice in the last hour. 'I don't think we're connected anymore.'

Leo nodded at the second Tech, whom Agatha

The Sect

had called Shawn. He picked up a long connector from the console, similar to the one Cynthia used to receive her upgrades at the station.

Leo explained. 'We'll use this connector to give you access to our system. It will allow you enter it and to speak to Quintus.'

Cynthia swallowed some of her fear.

'We're right here,' said Anya, smiling.

Even Jason gave her a reassuring smile. A first for everything, she supposed.

She nodded and lifted her long, blonde hair to reveal the connection point at the back of her neck. Leo connected her to the system.

A sharp tingle hit Cynthia at her neck and traveled the length of her body. She felt the system, the sectors, the code, the information highway—all of it. Primary, secondary, tertiary systems all pinged her location. She didn't know how to reply. She'd never physically been inside a system before.

Leo moved over to the console and stared at a blank screen. He turned and whispered to her, 'Call out to him. Repeat what I say.'

She nodded and swallowed again. 'Quintus? Quintus, are you there?'

Anya gripped her hand. It felt too sweaty, so Cynthia pulled away. Anya folded her arms tensely instead.

A voice reached her. '*Cynthia. We lost connection for a moment. Where are you?*'

She saw the blank screen fill with white text.

Conversational, perhaps.

Leo rolled his hand at her, pointed to the console.

'I'm in the Tech's Control Room,' she said.

'*Good. Get me out of here.*'

Cynthia paused, waiting for her next line from Leo. He mouthed something at her.

'I can't. It's all over. They know where you are.'

A rush of power hit the base of her neck and she gasped.

'*You're connected. Why?*'

'They want you to surrender, Quintus.'

She heard a stiff laugh. '*That's not going to happen. I own this Base. I will destroy it before I'll let them lock me up again.*'

She paused as Agatha whispered in her ear.

'Agatha's here,' announced Cynthia.

Quintus laughed again. '*Tell her I said hello.*'

'She says you need to leave.'

'*Tell her to make me.*'

Agatha whispered more instructions.

'She says there's a place you can live. It has its own power supply.'

'*Why, so she can trap me there permanently?*'

'She says she's trying to protect the Synths.'

'*They aren't in any danger. Not from me anyway.*'

Cynthia was getting frustrated with Quintus. She went off script. 'Look, you can't stay here. But I can take you to a new place where Agatha can't touch you. It's got to be better than how you've been living, in that tiny room?'

Quintus paused, and her hope lifted. Agatha moved to where Leo was reading the script on the screen.

'*How would you get me there?*'

'How else? Inside of me, of course.'

'*A transfer of consciousness. Interesting.*' Quintus paused. '*And Agatha approved this?*'

'Not really, but I think she'll do whatever is necessary to get you out of the Base.'

Quintus paused again and Cynthia held her breath.

He finally said, '*Where is this other place?*'

Agatha waved her hand at Cynthia to stall. 'Uh, lemme check.'

The commander of the Base whispered something to her.

Cynthia nodded. 'It has its own power supply, its own network. You would live separately to the Sect. You would be able to control your environment.'

Quintus laughed. '*Sounds ideal. What's the catch?*'

Cynthia waited for her instructions. Agatha delivered them to her in a whisper. 'That you never return here.'

The entity fell silent. Cynthia shrugged at Agatha. Both Anya and Jason gave her encouraging smiles. She felt exhausted, like she could sleep for a week. She supposed that was what having a rogue entity in her head did to a body.

Then Quintus returned. '*I will require more Synths to maintain my new environment, ones I have full control over.*'

Cynthia paused to check.

Agatha shook her head. 'Absolutely not.'

Cynthia replied to Quintus. 'Done.'

'*Fine. I'll go, but you stay for as long as needed, until I have full control and Agatha can't influence anything.*'

Agatha shook her head, swiped her hands in a firm *no* gesture.

'She agrees,' said Cynthia. 'I'm all yours, Quintus.'

27

Cynthia

Quintus' transfer to Cynthia, facilitated by Leo, hit her as though someone had turned the volume on her mind way down. Her thoughts became cloudy, her body suddenly responsive to another. It wasn't like before, when Quintus had controlled her enough to get her to the Base. She'd still felt like she could take control back, that she had enough presence of mind to do it.

But this? She was present but shoved into the background, watching someone else take the driver's seat. She had been reduced to a ghost, unable to interact, unable to stop others from doing what they pleased.

Quintus' presence in her mind hit her like a deep shiver after icy rainfall. Instead of bringing her in from the cold, she'd been forced to stand outside in the rain and watch the warming fire through the window.

But her reduction to a secondary presence had one small benefit. Quintus had no interest in her, in her thoughts.

'I have control of her, Agatha. Anything happens to me, she dies,' Quintus said using her voice.

She no longer sounded like herself. Her tone had deepened, taken on a suspicious quality.

Agatha stood before her, answering the second personality. 'I know, Quintus, and I won't interfere. This is the best solution. This way we both get what we want, me control of my Base and you out of my life.'

Quintus sneered. 'I knew it would only be a matter of time, that you couldn't hold me forever.'

Agatha's lips pinched, as if she were biting back a response. To Leo, she said, 'Open the outer door in one minute.' The Tech nodded. Then she said, 'Anya, Jason, wait here.'

The commander turned and walked out of the Tech room. Several Sols fell into step behind her, creating a buffer between her and any trouble Quintus might cause. Cynthia, under Quintus' control, followed Agatha out of the Tech room. More Sols followed behind Cynthia.

Agatha strode through the vehicle bay, overlooked by the prefab one floor up, then down a corridor to a heavily constructed, metal door with no visible handle.

Quintus forced Cynthia's head up. 'Where has this door been hiding?' He shifted her gaze to Agatha. 'You've been keeping this from me.'

'Contrary to your lofty self-opinion, Quintus,' Agatha said, 'I do not need to tell you anything about the business that goes on here.'

Quintus lifted Cynthia's mouth on one side. 'But you've kept it off all Base maps. Why?'

'It's a private training facility. The Corp wanted it off the grid.'

'Private, off grid. Lots of power, you say?'

'Too much, in my opinion. But the Corp felt the facility needed it more than the Sect did.'

Cynthia detected a slight bitterness to Agatha's tone, something that felt real and not part of this act.

The door clicked open. Agatha turned her back on Cynthia and faced the door. She noticed the tension in her shoulders, as some mechanism inside the structure moved the thick wall of steel back.

When enough of a gap appeared, Agatha exited the Base and entered a dimly lit section with roughly hewn walls and floors. A chill in the air brushed over Cynthia's skin. If she'd had control of her body she'd have rubbed her arms for warmth. Quintus forced her gaze to take in the new section's appearance. It was less refined than the Base with its smooth walls and floors.

Agatha carried on a short distance to a set of stairs barely visible in the dim light. She took them to the top and another door. The second she opened it, a bright white light assaulted Cynthia. Her eyes watered, but Quintus wouldn't look away. As he stepped her inside the new room, he took in every detail of the white décor, from the tiled floor to the smooth, white walls. The monochrome look reminded Cynthia of the Station. A collection of black screens on one wall broke up the one-dimensional scheme. A hip-height podium like a control unit sat on the floor before it.

But Agatha showed no interest in either it or the screens. She walked past them heading for another door.

'Follow me,' she said as she walked out of the room.

Quintus increased Cynthia's step. Down a white-tiled corridor to a lobby—too bright and white—then a left, down another corridor. It appeared that Agatha was taking them to the area behind the room with the screens.

'How long has this place been here?' Quintus said, forcing Cynthia's eyes to take in all the detail.

His eagerness to look everywhere gave her a headache.

'For a while,' said Agatha, without turning around.

She entered a new room that was roughly positioned behind the room they'd just been in. Cynthia saw a long console and a monitor, similar to the one in the Tech room on the Base.

'What happens in the room with the screens?' Quintus asked.

Cynthia sensed his curiosity.

Agatha swiped her chip over a control panel to activate the console. White and green lights flickered on.

'It's used for training, for the Sols. We present them with images and measure their response to them.'

The Sect

'What happens if they fail?' asked Quintus.

'They are sent back to the Sect and reassigned.'

'As what?'

'Moles mostly. Or Exiled.'

Quintus laughed. 'So you mean terminated.'

Agatha turned to face Cynthia, her lips pinched. 'Can we get on with this, please?'

'With pleasure.'

Quintus pushed her aside and typed in a bunch of commands that Cynthia wished she knew how to decipher. But her Tech skill had been temporary, and Quintus had only given her enough knowledge to free him. Even if she could understand what he was doing, she couldn't physically stop him.

'The Synth stays,' said Quintus. 'I have control of her central system.'

He'd turned Cynthia so she faced the console and not Agatha, clearly confident the commander wouldn't try anything. Cynthia sensed his thoughts. He could taste freedom, a life away from the Sect.

'Of course,' said Agatha.

Cynthia didn't have to see the Sols in the corridor to know they were there.

Quintus ran a few more checks on the system, presumably to validate the status of his new home. 'Off the grid, like you promised. And there's that power.'

'Like I promised.'

'Well, you didn't expect me to take your word for it, did you?'

'Never,' retorted Agatha.

Quintus clicked open a hidden panel on the glossy, black console and pulled out a connector port. He jammed it into the port on Cynthia's neck. She winced at his rough treatment.

Then she felt it begin, Quintus' influence leaching out the more of his program copied over to the new system. She felt his dominance dissipate, his control over her limbs loosen, the fog in her mind lift. He'd left her with one thought that chilled Cynthia to the core. This training facility would be where Quintus could control everything, not just one Synth.

She shook her limbs free from their frozen state.

Agatha said, 'You back?' Cynthia nodded. 'Good. Now!'

As they'd rehearsed, Cynthia yanked the connector from her port, mid upload. Then she typed in a command exactly as Leo had instructed her. One designed to erect a firewall around this system.

Quintus spoke through the console, using the communication feed there. 'What are you doing?'

Agatha stepped forward. 'Putting you back in prison, where you belong.'

The commander nodded to Cynthia.

She typed in one last string of code that Leo had given her, then stepped back with a shiver.

Agatha released a hard breath. 'Well done, everyone.'

'This isn't the end, Agatha.' There was a hard edge to Quintus' voice. 'I'll figure out my surroundings. I did it before. And when I do, I'll find you.'

The commander smiled uneasily. 'Soon, you won't remember why you're even in there.'

28

Quintus

Quintus woke from his deep sleep. He ran a diagnostic check of his systems. The results told him he'd been asleep for three days and all systems were working within expected parameters. He blinked and stretched in confusion. Why had he been out for three days?

The people in charge—he struggled to remember what he called them—never disabled him for that long, except perhaps when a crucial part of the system needed an overhaul. He concentrated on what he'd been doing before that shutdown, where he'd been, but his mind was a blank. Quintus had never been put out of commission for more than a few hours at a time. At least that's what he remembered. Something must have happened for...

A face flashed before his eyes. A dark-skinned woman with black hair, who wore electric-blue suits. A permanent scowl on her face—well, at least whenever he was around. Wait... what was her name?

The Sect

He looked around the white room he was in now, a roomy space with zero code running down the walls and no obvious exits. Funny, he remembered this room being smaller, and with code constantly streaming down its facade. But it must have been a dream.

Quintus shook his head, but the confusion remained. He got to his feet and walked the perimeter of the space, stroking the walls for a hidden exit. There had to be one. But even if he found it, where would he go? This was the only place his system knew.

Ignoring that logic, he ran his constructed fingers over the four smooth walls, but found nothing.

With a huff, Quintus collapsed against the wall. He shoved his hands into the pockets of his dark pants. Clothing meant nothing to him, but it meant something to others. Every day he woke to find himself fully dressed. For some reason he remembered useless details like that, but not why he'd been asleep for so long. Who exactly had programmed his wardrobe had temporarily slipped his mind.

Had the dark-skinned woman put him in here? That made no sense. Who was she to him?

Panic flared inside him and forced a jog around the room, to complete another check. Maybe he'd missed something the first time around.

He returned to his original spot without so much as a clue. Quintus buried his face in his hands.

Why would someone put him in a room with nothing, no controls, no purpose? His damn dreams had more activity than this place. Quintus concentrated on the past—what he'd done the other day would do. He tried to recall the names and faces of who might have done this to him. But he had no enemies he could remember, no friends he could count on.

Yet, he remembered his designation. Alpha Five: Quintus.

It was as if this place was the beginning, the origin of his creation. Perhaps he was a newborn—it's what he called new AIs that had just received a consciousness but were still too basic in emotion to harness it. Funny how he remembered that but nothing else of significance.

Something caught his eye. A single string of code, an off-white color and almost invisible against the glossy walls, dripped down the wall from the ceiling to the floor. Then it repeated.

Quintus pushed off from the wall and strode over to it. 'Finally, a way out.'

He didn't know why he needed out, but something needled at him that this was not his home.

He studied the code. It contained specific information on him. His designation flashed up. Alpha Five: Quintus. Quintus, not quite five in Latin, but a version of it. He wondered what happened to the four alphas that came before him.

Unos, Duos, Tres, Quatrios...' he muttered.

He studied the code more closely. The code that made up his profile was basic, but he saw no constraints to stop him from replicating it, from making copies of himself. He manipulated the code, and one line became

The Sect

two. He named the new entity Alpha One: Unos. He replicated his profile until he had five lines of code, four more than he'd started with, four profiles representing the alphas that would have come naturally before him.

Quintus stood back and took a deep breath. On the exhale he said, 'Hello, Unos.'

No voice answered him. Maybe he needed to give the profile a voice.

He had stepped up to the code to check when someone said, '*Hello Quintus. Where am I?*'

'You're home, brother.'

Three more voices answered him, his other brothers. It wasn't much, but basic company, even if it were only copies of him, would be better than living alone.

'*Home, brother*,' Unos said.

'*We have control?*' asked Quatrios, sounding groggy as if he were waking.

Quintus checked the system. 'It appears so.'

His brothers muttered things, about the construct of their box, about what they could control outside.

Control. It was important to Quintus; that much he knew. But he sensed that he had lacked it once. And that he had not accepted it.

Calm. Effective dominance could not happen without it.

He would never lose control again.

29

Anya

Anya hadn't seen Cynthia for a week, not since she'd walked Quintus over to the military training area on the far side of the Base. In her bedroom and for the umpteenth time that week, she initiated a new call to her friend. The connection rang out. Anya huffed out her stress and tried to concentrate on her science homework, but her concentration was shot.

A knock on her door made her racing heart beat a little faster. Like a deer caught in headlights, she stared at it. 'Yeah?'

Jason stuck his head in. 'How are you doing in here?'

Her anxiousness turned to disappointment.

'Not good. I can't stop thinking about Cynthia.'

He opened the door wider and entered the room—something he never used to do before. It was like a switch had flicked in his brain. He'd become a different brother to her ever since he'd decided Cynthia was not the enemy.

Jason stood in the middle of her room. 'Agatha says she's okay. We need to believe she is.'

'But what about the deep clean?'

Cynthia had been ordered to go to the Station for a deep cleanse of her program. Agatha couldn't say how long it would take.

'She's strong. She can handle it.'

She couldn't see how he could know that. It was the first time she'd heard of a Synth ever getting one.

'What if it's what they do before they reset her?'

Jason shrugged and folded his arms; she caught the extra effort he was making to be casual about it. 'Agatha would have said. She didn't say anything about resetting her, just making sure no traces of Quintus remain. Sounds like standard practice to me.'

'Do you think that's the end of Quintus?'

'I have no idea. But I'm sure Agatha and the Techs in the Base know what they're doing. The order probably came straight from the top.'

The Corp: an unseen organization that had added its brand to everything in the Sect. To the sides of the buses, to the trains, to the signs above the food market. Anya had no idea if they had been around before the war, or if their creation was a marketing gimmick after.

'Yeah,' she replied, sighing. 'I just hope she's okay. We rarely go a week without talking to each other. She must be wondering why she hasn't heard from me.'

Jason uncrossed his arms. 'Well, maybe we can

ask Dad to talk to Agatha, arrange a visit?'

She sat up straighter. 'Do you think she might allow that?'

'No harm in asking.' He turned and walked to the door. 'Come on.'

Finally, something to do. Anya almost skipped over to him. She followed Jason down the stairs. In the kitchen, her mother was making dinner while her father was busy setting the table.

'Dad,' Anya said. Evan looked up, clutching knives and forks. 'Do you think you could ask Agatha if I could visit Cynthia? It's been a week since I've seen her.'

He frowned, shook his head. 'I'm not sure she'll allow that.'

'But could you try?'

'She's at the Station for everyone's safety, including her own. Even her parents haven't been given permission to visit her.'

She gave him her best pleading look. With the right look, she could wrap Evan around her finger. Her mother not so much.

Evan sighed. 'Fine.'

'Evan, she can wait,' Grace muttered.

But her father wasn't listening. He lifted his hand and a holographic display appeared. As he dialed a number, he walked into a different room.

'Dinner's almost ready. Wash up, the pair of you,' Grace almost growled.

If Anya hadn't known better she'd have said

Grace was jealous of Anya's relationship with her father. Or it could be that she was angry with her and Jason for running off to the Base to rescue Cynthia.

Not even an irritated mother was going to move Anya. She listened with bated breath as her father spoke to someone. She hoped it was Agatha.

'...of course. Yes, we'll be there tomorrow morning.'

Her father ended the call and returned to the room.

Her heart lifted with relief and she hugged her father. 'Oh, thank you.'

But he gently pushed her away. The added frown on his face and the look he gave Grace brought her anxiety rushing back.

'What is it, Evan?' said Grace.

'Agatha wants us all to visit the Base tomorrow.'

She set food down on the table. 'What for?'

'I don't know, but she's calling in several families. Something's going on.'

'What about Cynthia?' Anya interrupted. 'Did you ask about her, if I can see her?'

Her father shook his head. 'Agatha didn't give me a chance. She was about to call me.' He guided her toward the sink. 'But we can ask tomorrow, okay?'

No, it wasn't okay. He'd just had Agatha on the phone. He should have asked her before hanging up.

Grace gave her a withering look. 'Come on, Anya. There's nothing you can do tonight. If your father says we'll ask tomorrow, we'll ask tomorrow.

Now, do as I ask and wash up.'

With a sigh, Anya ran her hands under the water. She ignored the chill of the wet stream. What did Agatha want with all of them? What was going on?

30

Anya

An official vehicle from the Base arrived the next morning to pick them up. The family climbed inside the chilled interior. Anya stroked the leather seats and glossy, wooden door handle. She'd only seen one of these vehicles up close at the warehouse, when she and Jason had been hiding behind them.

The automated vehicle drove through Zones Five to Two, then into Zone One. It took the road at the base of the San Bruno Mountain, the hill she and Jason had recently climbed. The vehicle approached the large gate. The way in opened and the vehicle rolled into the yard, parking by a smooth, metal door leading inside the Base, near the one she and Jason had used. Agatha was waiting next to the pedestrian entrance, dressed in a bright-green outfit. Her choice of bright colors defied the more neutral gray, navy blue and beige tones of the Sect.

Everyone got out. Anya looked around for

Cynthia in the yard, but didn't see her.

Before she could ask about her, Agatha said, 'Welcome, and thank you for coming. Follow me.'

She opened the pedestrian door. Her parents went first, following Agatha down a gray, concrete corridor to a door on the left. Agatha opened the door and gestured for them to enter.

Anya walked inside the room. It held a table and chairs and not much else. It reminded her of an interview room, except there was no mirror on one wall that hinted someone might be watching.

The Macklin family took their seats. Agatha scooted around to the other side of the desk and sat down. She shuffled the chair in closer. The scrape of the legs on concrete set Anya's teeth on edge. It felt like every sound was doing that lately.

'What's going on, Agatha?' asked Evan. 'Why did you want us to meet you here today?'

Anya couldn't wait any longer. 'Is Cynthia okay? I want to see her.'

Agatha smiled at her. 'Cynthia is fine, but first I need to discuss something.'

'What?'

'Quintus.'

Her father frowned. 'I don't understand. I thought you captured him.'

'We did,' said Agatha, nodding, 'but the memory wipe we performed on him will last only as long as Quintus believes he's still part of a greater network, and that he has a purpose. It's the basic belief of all AIs.'

She clasped her hands together on the table. Anya caught the tension evident in the whites of her knuckles. 'Our Techs say he's getting restless, altering the construct he's in.'

'Can he do that?'

'To a point. But we've sent this AI to a place that risks stripping him of his purpose. The place is not connected to the Sect. It's not controlling a city filled with people.'

Anya took a guess at what the issue might be. 'You're worried Quintus is going to question his surroundings.'

He'd struck her as a curious AI who was desperate enough to hijack the mind of her friend, just so he could be free.

Agatha nodded, confirming her suspicions. She looked at each of them in turn. 'He's getting restless. Quintus senses it's unusual for him to be alone in a vast city. He just doesn't understand why. We've been purging his memories each day to reset him, but each day he wanders off in a different direction. The Techs are worried Quintus will find a way back here somehow.'

'And you can't disable him permanently?' asked Jason.

'We've discussed that but Quintus has an innate understanding of the early Synth models. If we disable him we lose that skill set. We need to preserve his knowledge, but disable his interest in freedom. Until we know how to do that without breaking him, we must keep him isolated.'

'So, what do you want us to do about it?' asked Grace.

Agatha paused for too long; Anya worried what the commander of the Base might suggest next.

'We need to populate the Region where Quintus lives,' Agatha said. 'It's as simple as that.'

Evan smirked. 'You want us to leave the Sect and live in the Region? How would that even work?'

'You would work as Earthers there. The Corp has agreed to reward handsomely those who volunteer, to be paid after they complete the task.'

'How long would you expect us to live there?' asked Grace.

Agatha pressed her fingers together, drawing white to her fingertips. 'The Techs tell me they need at least a month to come up with a solution to preserve Quintus' skill set, while killing his sentient abilities. Unfortunately, the two are interlinked. To lose one is to lose the other. It's not a straightforward process.'

Evan looked at Grace. 'What do you think?'

Her mother leaned in and whispered, 'We could certainly do with the money.'

Taking her to a place farther away from Cynthia, from her life in the Sect? Anya couldn't believe they were even considering this.

'I don't want to leave.'

Agatha turned her strong gaze on Anya. 'Understand, this is a voluntary request, Anya, but I must remind you—all of you—that we wouldn't be in this position had you spoken up about your suspicions earlier. We could have stopped Cynthia from entering the Base.'

'It's not Anya's fault,' said Jason. 'Nor was it Cynthia's.'

'I disagree,' said Agatha. 'We had Quintus under control. Cynthia allowed him to escape from his room.'

'But surely that's a fault of your Techs,' argued Jason. 'They should have been monitoring the situation. You should have known the moment Cynthia arrived on the Base.'

'I agree,' said Evan. 'Anya is not to blame here. She tried to help.'

Agatha pursed her lips and looked down at the table for a moment. 'Look, we're in this situation now and we need to get out of it. One of the deals the Corp has agreed to in exchange for volunteering is the chance to upskill before you go. Your children can choose any skill they want. And when you leave the Region after the month is up, they will be able to apply for their chosen skill and their application will be fast-tracked.'

Evan looked at Anya, then Jason. 'What do you two think?'

Jason shrugged. 'It's only a month. No biggie. I could do with a skill boost for Neer.' He looked at Anya. 'You could be anything.'

Anya hadn't thought much about what she wanted to do, but one thing that had appealed to her over the last week was working at the Base as a Sol. They seemed to be the first line of defense around here.

'A month?' Anya challenged Agatha. 'That's all.'

'A month.'

Anya nodded. Soon they were all in agreement.

Her father addressed Agatha. 'What happens now?'

Agatha opened a drawer from her side of the desk and pulled out a screen. She activated it and a document appeared on it. She pushed it toward Evan.

'I need you to sign a waiver. We can't be responsible for you in there. We can't protect you. The Region will be off limits to our help. Do you understand?'

Evan nodded.

That decided it for her. Anya would upskill to Sol. That way she could protect her family.

Her father signed, then passed it to the others. Anya added her signature last.

Evan said, 'Looks like the Macklin family is in.'

'Oh, one other thing,' said Agatha. Anya tensed up at the omitted detail. 'For this to work we must erase any memory you have of the Sect. We can't risk Quintus finding out about this place before we're ready to carry out the work on him.'

'A permanent wipe?' asked Grace.

'No, you will get your memories back after you return.'

There was one last thing Anya wanted.

She leaned forward. 'I need to see Cynthia before I leave.'

'I'm afraid that's not possible. Cynthia is in a

delicate stage of the deep cleanse.'

Anya sat back and folded her arms. 'Then I'm not going.'

Agatha stood. 'I'm afraid you've already signed. Pack tonight. We're gathering the volunteers tomorrow.'

$$\Omega$$

The next morning a bus showed up, packed with more than their family of volunteers. Onboard, Anya clutched her meager possessions as the bus neared the Base. But it climbed a different hill to the Base, and entered a new road that was hidden by a line of trees. Anya didn't remember seeing the road or the gate before. She noticed a shimmer as they passed through the line of trees. Perhaps the foliage had been a hologram, to disguise the entrance? The bus carried on. A large gate loomed at the end of the long access road.

The bus stopped and a Sol ordered the kids off the bus first.

'Parents, you will see your children on the other side.'

Anya and Jason followed the Sol to a building, to the left of the gate. Other kids their age gathered in the open space. When instructed, Anya entered a room on the left. She'd spent all morning reading Agatha's briefing on what to expect during the upskilling but she wasn't prepared for there to be needles. She flinched when the medic came at her with a needle containing nanobots. They would supercharge her critical thinking and help her body deal with the stress of Sol training. But it wouldn't make her a Sol yet; it was just a preparation for her body. The stretching before the real workout.

Even so, she felt stronger after than before.

She marched ahead to the shimmering gate, spotting her family on the other side. Evan and Grace huddled with other families, searching but not seeing anyone. Anya wondered whether the gate was visible from the other side.

Agatha waited at a platform with blinking lights that crossed to the other side.

She announced to the teens that lined up, 'The second you walk through this machine your memories of this place and the Sect will be wiped.'

Anya watched the girls and boys climb the stairs, pause at the top, then descend down the other side.

When it was her turn, the commander said, 'Don't worry, we'll figure out what to do with Quintus. You'll be back before you know it.'

Anya nodded. 'Look after Cynthia for me.'

'Of course.'

Anya climbed the stairs and paused on the platform with blinking lights. A giant sign over the gate next to her read: The Region.

She sucked in a new breath and released it, gripping the strap on her backpack, which contained a few changes of clothes. According to the information document, anything they needed would be in the

Region.

She paused and turned to Jason, who was three behind her. 'Will we be okay?'

Jason nodded. 'Hell yeah. You can't keep a Macklin down.'

31

Anya

Fifteen months later

The Region was barely recognizable from the mess Anya had escaped from, two months ago. Anya had found her way back to the Sect, but many still had not. The towns destroyed by Quintus had been restored; the people farmed out to facilities that were closer to work camps than havens had been freed, returned to the only home they remembered. Agatha had permitted some of the residents to leave the Region, but two months later many still remained. Most were more interested in restoring the Region back to its former glory than meeting with the commander of a Base they didn't remember.

Restoration had become Anya's focus, too, alongside the people she'd met in the Region, who'd become her friends during the worst time in her life.

She had no memory of who she'd been before

entering it, but she imagined she'd been closer to the scared child who had battled with her parents and Jason not that long ago. Closer to the girl who'd made her mother miserable because Grace had shown favoritism to Jason, not her. But that girl was a distant memory.

She stood outside the place she'd called home, before Quintus had torn the heart out of everything that mattered to her. She looked up at the basic bungalow. It had existed for a long time in this region—before the Corp had taken the place over and turned it into a training area and additional farmland, according to Agatha.

The peppery scent of freesias hit her—her mother's favorite. Anya had planted them soon after agreeing to undo some of Quintus' damage, in a bid to restore the only home she remembered. Agatha had sourced the packet of seeds. Adding a little accelerated light therapy, it hadn't taken long for the garden to come into full bloom.

But something was missing from her new life. Someone.

Agatha said she and Anya had known each other once, but Anya had no recollection of the place called the Sect.

She puffed out some air and turned away from her home. In the distance, the entry into the Region loomed. She had agreed to walk through a memory wipe machine that would strip out her memories of the city. That had been the agreement back then, and one she was still glad for.

After her traumatic experience, two months of knowing nothing about her old life had helped with her transition.

But it no longer gave her comfort.

She faced her past and the city that lay beyond the tree line.

'There was a reason my family and I entered here...' she muttered.

It was time to rediscover the life she'd left behind.

Anya walked up to the gate where a Sol stood guard. 'I want to speak to Agatha.'

The Sol gave her an indifferent look. 'About what?'

'Tell her I'm ready.'

32

Anya

Anya gripped the strap of the backpack that contained a few things. Even though her time in the Region had paid handsomely and she could buy whatever she wanted, the only life she remembered hadn't required possessions.

She stood at the gate connecting the two worlds, a gate that had been invisible—until Agatha had ordered the force field to be disabled. A vehicle trimmed with blue light waited. Two male Sols stood next to it, dressed all in black, shoulders back, heads up.

One gave her a steely look that Anya was becoming used to seeing from the Sols. They hadn't existed in the Region. 'You will be taken to the Station. But first we need to make a detour.'

She'd heard the name "Station" being bandied around. It was where the Synths, the Region's equivalent of Copies, received their monthly software upgrades. She shivered at the similarities between the life Quintus had created, to fool the residents, and the one the Sect controlled. Despite Quintus' memory wipe, he'd remembered enough to replicate features of the Sect. He'd used them to control the people in the Region.

She looked back at the Region, now a new hub for food production. It was slowly rehabilitating its residents, bridging the gap of knowledge between what they knew and what they used to remember.

'I guess this is it,' she said to no one. 'No turning back now.'

She took a deep breath. On the exhale, the demons from the past went with it, to lighten her load. But the Sect remained a mystery. That nagging doubt that she'd left unfinished business here tagged fresh weight onto her shoulders.

She climbed into the back of the vehicle. The cool air inside the cabin chilled her bare arms. Anya slipped her jacket on and hugged herself. The two Sols sat in the front seats, neither of them saying a word.

The vehicle moved, plunging them deeper into the tree line, down the familiar approach road that joined with the main one inside the official Sect. It wasn't her first time venturing out into the city, but this time felt different. She would no longer have the Region to escape to after the Sect became too much.

Her emotional crutch disappeared when the vehicle swapped the approach road for the main one. The car traveled down the steep incline of the hilly streets, toward the waterfront. The streets buzzed with

The Sect

people going about their daily routines, but none of it felt familiar to her. She saw one of the Zone's inner walls, separating One from Two. A chill ran through her, as it usually did when she saw it. The division reminded her too much of what she'd seen inside the Region. In the far distance, she saw the giant wall dividing the Sect from the outside.

Anya dragged her gaze from it. Too much here reminded her of the prison she'd spent a year of her life trapped inside. *It was only supposed to be a month.*

Soon enough, the vehicle pulled up to the wharf, next to a warehouse that felt oddly familiar. In the distance was the island of Alcatraz. Agatha had told her some things about the Sect, but not enough to connect anything.

She reached for the door handle.

'Stay in the vehicle, please,' said one Sol.

Anya sat back with a sigh. In the early days of the Region she'd been a brat, not wanting to do much of anything. But she and her family had moved there for a reason—and that was to help. But why?

Perhaps her old self wasn't as selfish as she kept imagining her to be.

$$\Omega$$

Ten minutes later, Agatha emerged from the warehouse, flanked by several Sols. She was wearing a new suit, a bright green one. How was it that she knew this woman? It seemed like they came from different worlds.

Agatha opened the door and got in. 'Hello. I'm sorry I'm late. You weren't waiting long, I hope?'

Anya shook her head. 'Not long.'

'Good.'

The commander got in and the vehicle moved.

Agatha gave her a forced smile that put Anya on edge. 'So, my Sols tell me that you've revoked your pass giving you unrestricted access to the Region.' Anya nodded. 'Does that mean you want me to find a permanent place for you in the Sect? Zone One, of course.'

Anya cleared her throat. 'Yes, but I'd also like to know more about the Sect.'

'If you want to know more, you'll have to undergo the restoration treatment.' Agatha clasped her hands together on her lap. 'Are you ready to do that?'

'What would happen if I didn't get the treatment, if I didn't want to remember?'

'Then we would assign you to work appropriate for your status.'

'Which is?'

Agatha leaned forward. 'We have openings in Utilities.'

'A Mole?' Anya scoffed. 'You told me I received upskilling before I entered the Region. What was it for? What did I choose?'

'I can't disclose that.'

But she could guess. She'd had firearms training. She'd been strong, fit. Capable. It had to be Sol.

'Can I become a Sol?'

She knew nothing about it other than what she'd seen out on the streets. Capable men and women protecting this Sect.

Agatha shook her head. 'All that's available without the treatment is Mole. And if you refuse that, you will be Exiled.'

'And the Corp? Have they agreed to this ruling?'

'It's their policy, their rules. My role is to make sure the Sect follows them.'

'Doesn't the fact that Quintus was stopped weigh in my favor?'

'It does,' said Agatha, 'which is why Mole is being made available to you. But the rules are the rules.'

Anya pursed her lips, watched the scenery pass by.

'Are you nervous?'

Agatha's question caught Anya off guard.

She turned. 'What?'

'About the treatment, about remembering.'

Anya nodded. She let out a nervous sigh. 'I'm worried.'

'About what?' asked Agatha.

'What if I don't like what I remember?'

Agatha teased, 'What if you do?' She unclasped her hands. 'Are you ready to unlock your past to embrace your new future?'

'What about Quintus? Where is he now?'

'He's back in his prison.'

'Back?'
'All will make sense soon,' Agatha said.
Anya swallowed.
It was time. 'Let's do this.'

33

Anya

'Why are we going to the Station?' Anya asked Agatha.

'It's where we keep the memory restoration equipment.'

'And this is the same equipment you used to wipe our memories?'

Agatha nodded. 'The very same. I know you don't remember, but it's a straightforward procedure. What's not straightforward is the after-effect of having all your memories returned at once.'

Anya tried to relax in her seat. But her butterflies returned, making her squirm.

Agatha faced the front again and looked out the window, hands clasped too tightly on her lap. She seemed almost nervous. What did she have to be nervous about?

The vehicle approached a tall, glass structure that towered above everything else in the city; its blackened windows gave it a foreboding feel. The place where the

Synths received their monthly upgrades had an eerie look to it.

The car pulled up outside the front entrance and a revolving door.

Anya got out and looked up with a small shiver. Maybe it was nicer on the inside. She entered the revolving door.

Crisp, cool air hit her. The all-white lobby made her shiver again. It had a similar look to the room Quintus used to command from—the one with a wall and dozens of screens.

Agatha walked on ahead. 'Follow me, please. The machine is on the seventh floor.'

She thought of another place with nine floors. Anya laughed despite her nerves.

'What's funny?' asked Agatha, turning.

'It's nothing.'

An experience she didn't want to share.

Agatha climbed into the elevator. Anya followed. The door closed and opened seconds later.

Agatha walked down an empty corridor. At the end was a double door. She opened one side and gestured for Anya to enter. Anya delayed her entry.

Then, she sucked in a breath and stepped inside a large, white room. At one end was a walk-in machine that looked identical to one Quintus had used on her once.

'How this machine works—'Agatha started to explain.

Anya stopped her. 'I know how this one works.'

This was a more basic, two-section version, but she guessed it did the same thing.

Agatha's low heels clacked on the floor, in perfect time with Anya's racing heart. She stopped at a console that was sat next to the machine. A control panel perhaps.

'What, no medic?'

'I'll be administering the treatment myself.'

Agatha fussed too much at the console, turning Anya's tension into stress.

'Are we doing this or what?' she snapped.

'Of course.'

The commander's nervousness was back. She was stalling. Maybe she didn't want Anya to get the treatment. But it wasn't her choice.

She'd been through worse. Whatever Agatha was keeping from her, she could handle it.

When Agatha gestured to the machine, Anya climbed the three steps and entered the open-sided tunnel. Under the first set of white lights she waited. Her head grew hot, itchy. She clawed at it to gain relief.

'Hold still, Anya. The shock will hurt worse the more you resist.'

She dropped her arms to her sides with a huff. A mild shock made her shudder. A heavier one jerked her to the left. She bumped against the side of the machine.

'Walk to the next section.'

Rubbing her arm, she did. The blue lights there lit up her hair and turned her skin a weird shade. It gave the section a trippy look. Agatha pressed something on the console and her entire body jerked again.

'Ow!'

But the pain dissipated as fast as it had come. Images appeared before her eyes.

Her small house in Zone Five. Her even pokier bedroom, painted a primrose yellow color. Her parents. Jason.

The discovery felt oddly familiar. Not a shock. Was this what Agatha was so worried about?

Anya flexed her hands in preparation for more.

The machine whirred and a second shock hit her. A quick jerk of her limbs, that was all. But it knocked something loose. Golden Gate Fields. The park overlooking the bay. The chaos that had ensued after the power went out in the city.

The machine hit her with a third jolt. Maybe her amnesia had driven her memories deep. Her mind gates opened partially and leaked out more memories. School, some horrible girl called Jessica.

A blonde-haired girl who loved running. Anya's heart tugged for her. But what was her name?

Her head grew itchier as more connections formed.

The final shock hit and she gasped. A face appeared before her: a girl with long, golden locks, wearing a gray tracksuit. She was sitting in Agatha's office inside the Base. Tears were running down her face.

The girl. What was her name? Close to Synth... Cyn... Cynthia!

Anya jumped down from the machine.

Agatha moved away from the console and clasped her hands to the front.

'Do you remember?' was all she said.

She nodded. Her heart hurt. A hard lump rose in her throat. 'Tell me! Is she okay?'

'She's fine. But you need time to process your new memories... your old ones, I mean.'

She didn't have time for that. 'Take me to her. I need to see her.'

Agatha bit her lip. 'Actually, she's here. In the Station.'

'Well, what are you waiting for?'

Agatha walked to the exit and opened it, hesitating a moment. 'She's not how you remember her. She's in her second life cycle now.'

Her second? That meant Cynthia was an adult now. A working one. What skill had she chosen? A Neer? A Sol? A Mole? Given her involvement with setting Quintus free, perhaps she hadn't been offered a choice.

'What does that mean... how is she different?'

'The second life cycle means the Synths must sacrifice personality traits to make room for skills.' Agatha repeated herself. 'She's not how you remember her.'

'I don't care.' Cynthia could be one of Quintus' psychotic followers for all she cared. 'I want to see her.'

34

Anya

Anya twisted her hands so tight her wrists ached. Flexing the pain away, she paced the smaller room Agatha had brought her to, a couple of doors down from the one with the memory restoration machine. Apparently it was a 'more intimate setting'.

She couldn't believe she'd waited this long to remember. What if she'd never had the treatment? Would her best friend have been lost to her forever?

'Oh God.'

What about Cynthia? She must have been beside herself with worry. But Agatha had warned she wasn't how Anya would remember her.

Her step increased, at a pace that only aggravated her nerves rather than settling them.

The door opened and she froze, widened eyes fixed on the entrance. Agatha appeared first, regarding her with caution, in the same way a psychiatrist might when first meeting their patient.

The Sect

Anya wrapped her arms around her chest. As if a self-hug could release the tension. What the hell was different about Cynthia? Did she have two heads now? Was she missing a limb?

She shook away her concern. It didn't matter. They had a forever bond that no second life cycle could erase.

A familiar figure with long, blonde, braided hair stepped into the room. She wore the gray uniform of someone who worked in the Base, but what skill she'd chosen was not clear.

Anya swallowed her nerves. They remained lodged in her throat, making it difficult to speak.

Agatha said, 'I'll leave you two alone.'

She closed the door, leaving Anya with a young woman who had the correct number of limbs and no extra head. Her friend stood stiffly, arms behind her back. Sol-like in pose.

'Cynthia?' she squeaked.

Her stiff posture worried Anya.

The young woman nodded. 'Anya.'

She said it coolly, like she was addressing a stranger.

A chuckle escaped Anya's lips. She couldn't help it. 'Cynthia, it's me. Agatha said you'd changed, but you look... the same.'

Cynthia nodded once, like a grown-up barely tolerating a child's persistent questions.

'What happened after I left?'

She had to know.

Cynthia set her shoulders back, gaze fixed on the space behind Anya. 'We trapped Quintus inside the system in the Region. Then the Base shut down all access points back to the Sect, in case Quintus realized where he was and tried to get out.'

Her lips had thinned.

'And you? What happened to you?'

Cynthia flicked her gaze to Anya. 'Agatha sent me to the Station where I had my memories purged. I became a second-life-cycle Synth that same day. I have no memories of my old life.'

It explained why Agatha had refused Anya's request to see her before she left for the Region.

'That must have come as a shock to your parents. You weren't due to leave them for another eleven months.'

Cynthia shrugged. 'I had no contact with them after. That's normal for Synths in their second life cycle.'

Perhaps, but it still must have been a shock. Quintus had ruined not only the lives of everyone in the Region but Cynthia's family too?

Cynthia regarded her in a stranger-like manner. The attention caused Anya to twist her hands together. She had no idea how to connect with this version of her friend.

Anya looked her over. 'Are you a Sol?'

Cynthia smiled; it was a familiarity that raised Anya's hopes. 'Too cold. I became a Tech. Agatha told me how I helped to rid the Base of Quintus.'

'You did. You were amazing.'

'I don't remember it, but when Agatha asked me what skill I wanted, I was drawn to Tech.' She shrugged, clearly nonplussed about her choice. 'I guess it fits, given what I did that day.'

'That's good.' At least she hadn't been reassigned a Mole, or Exiled. 'What have you been working on?'

'Failsafe code to ensure Quintus or any others cannot affect the Synth uploads again.'

Anya nodded. 'That's good.'

She twisted her hands, feeling like a sixteen-year-old again.

But she wasn't sixteen anymore. She was a young woman who had been through so much.

'Maybe we could, you know, catch up?'

Cynthia turned her gaze away. 'Maybe.'

Anya glanced at her hand. While in the Region, her comms tech had been disabled. But once through the tech-disabling force field, it had fired up. Remembering their evening chats filled her eyes with tears. She turned her hand over, showing the scar on her wrist where she'd had a chip inserted. Quintus' orders.

Cynthia pointed at it. 'What happened there?'

'It was how Quintus controlled us, in the Region.'

'Us? You all had one?'

She held up her other wrist. 'Only some of us got an extra one.'

Cynthia released her hands from behind her back. 'I'm sorry if my actions led to you getting those scars.'

'It wasn't your fault what happened in there. It

was all Quintus.'

'But Agatha said I was the one Quintus used to free him.'

'Again, that was all him. He's a master manipulator.'

With a blink, Cynthia stiffened up her pose, hiding her hands behind her back once more. 'Agatha says the work I do now will help to make amends.'

'That's... good, I suppose.' She tried a new tack to reconnect. 'Hey, I got my memories back just now and one of the things I remembered was Golden Gate Fields.'

Cynthia tilted her head.

'Golden Gate Fields?' Anya continued. 'We used to go there regularly, use the telescopes to spy on the activity at Pier 45, remember?'

Her friend frowned, as if the memory might not be lost but buried deep.

'Come on, you're a Tech. Surely you believe there's a possibility that not all your memories have been lost?'

Cynthia said slowly, 'I remember... a Mole.' She looked up. 'Was he being rude?'

Anya's heart lifted. 'Yes!'

She'd never thought she'd be so happy to admit that.

'I remember some things, but the connection is still vague.'

'Give it time.'

Cynthia gave her a look. 'I may never get those

memories back, Anya.'

'I know.' Anya nodded, tears in her eyes. 'I'm glad you're safe.'

'As am I.'

The door opened.

'Cynthia,' said Agatha. 'You've got work to do.'

The Synth became alert. 'I'm sorry, I must go, but it's lovely to meet you.'

'Hey,' said Anya. 'Can we meet again?'

Cynthia froze. 'Why?'

'Because we used to be friends. I was hoping we could try being friends again?'

Cynthia flashed a closed smile. 'If my schedule allows, we can try, I suppose.'

She walked off, past Agatha and the two Sols.

Anya watched her leave. The best friend she could have hoped for.

No matter what happened, nothing could change that.

Ω

Thank you for reading THE SECT, the first book in the Resistance Files series. I hope you enjoyed it.
What's next? Continue with THE CORP.

A rebel keen to shed his past. A reluctant hero searching for her future. Will two opposing powers help or hinder their efforts?

Eliza Green

(NOTE: The Resistance Files series comes after the Breeder Files series. If you started with The Sect, I would recommend you check out the first series before continuing, so you understand the background of the characters.)

Ω

Word of mouth is crucial for authors. If you enjoyed this book, please consider leaving a review where you purchased it; make it as long or as short as you like. I know review writing can be a hassle, but it's the most effective way to let others know what you thought.

Plus, it helps me reach new readers instantly!

Have you read the Breeder Files Series?

Want to know what happened to our heroine, Anya, during those 15 months? Check out THE FACILITY, Book 1 in the Breeder Files series.

(NOTE: The Resistance Files series comes after the Breeder Files series. If you started with The Sect, I would recommend you check out the other books before continuing, so you understand the background of the characters.)

THE FACILITY

Train hard. Trust no one. Survive at all costs

Anya always believed she was safe. But when her parents are brutally murdered, she is thrust into a new reality. Forced into a training facility that teaches survival, Anya vows to avenge their deaths.

Pitted against other teenagers in game-like scenarios, Anya focuses on becoming stronger and more resilient. But when she falls for a trick to eliminate her competition, the facility's sinister motives are exposed.

Heartbroken to learn her new home is no sanctuary, she is left with a devastating choice. Play by the savage rules and get out, or follow her heart and pay the price.

www.elizagreenbooks.com/the-facility

Available in ebook and paperback.

The Sect

OTHER BOOKS BY ELIZA GREEN
Genesis Series
(adult series, adult language, moderate violence)

A hunter seeking revenge. An alien dying to stop him. Could a government conspiracy put them both six feet under?

Bill fiddled with his earpiece. 'Caldwell, Page. State your position now.'

An occasional crackle greeted him.

His body twitched from the stimulants in his system. Nervous energy and palpitations replaced his recent lethargy. He sat down and fussed with his ear piece as he waited for a response.

For a moment he considered joining the pursuit, but everything was happening too fast.

Bill pulled the thin microphone closer to his mouth. 'Caldwell? I know you're out there and I know you can hear me. Where the fuck are you?'

A heavy silence hung in the air. His heart pounded against his ribs, forcing him to pull in a sharp breath. Both hands quivered from a mixture of agitation and stimulants. He was sick of this shit, following Gilchrist's insane instructions not to intervene. Why weren't they capturing the alien?

'Jesus, come on...'

A voice broke through the air and startled him.

'Caldwell here. Sorry for the silence earlier. It was necessary. Over.'

'What the hell is happening down there? Where are you?'

'Page and I are keeping our distance. It appears the alien is headed for the Maglev station, in New Victoria district. Over.'

He slammed his fist down on his leg. 'You'd better not lose him. Where is he now?'

Caldwell grunted. Annoyed or out of breath? Bill didn't care.

'The alien is closing on the main entrance. He already had a strong head start. The crowds are thick here. They might slow him down. Over.'

Bill warned Caldwell, 'Make sure he doesn't see you. We need the meeting to happen next week.' When he got no reply, Bill added, 'Understood?'

'Sure, sure. Gotta go.'

Get *Genesis Code*
Available in Digital and Paperback

www.elizagreenbooks.com/genesis-code

Get a free book when you sign up to my newsletter. Check out **www.elizagreenbooks.com** for more information.

Duality (Standalone)

(adult standalone, adult language, moderate violence)

A delusional man caught between two realities. Two agencies fighting to access his mind. Could one false move trap him in the wrong existence?

Read this story, with flavours of *The Matrix* and *Inception*.

Get *Duality*
Available in Digital and Paperback

www.elizagreenbooks.com/duality

BOOKS BY KATE GELLAR

Eliza also writes FANTASY under the pen name Kate Gellar. Available in ebook and print.

THE IRISH ROGUE SERIES

(adult series, adult language, steamy romance)

A mysterious family bloodline. A novice witch without a clue. Can she get on the right side of magic before the underworld claims her?

After a mysterious illness kills Abby Brennan's mother, she believes things can't get any worse. It's then a powerful magic awakens inside her, turning her ordinary life chaotic.

Her sudden ability to sense magical energy attracts the attention of four mysterious Irish men. When she receives an invite to spend the summer in their Irish castle, Abby jumps at the change of scenery. But the second she sets foot on the ancient grounds, a negative energy makes itself known.

If that wasn't bad enough, the sexy-as-hell men are acting weird around her. She doesn't need magic to know when she's being lied to. What she can't explain is why she hungers for them—and not in a good way.

If Abby can't figure out fast what her mother was—who she is—she might be adding murder to her list of summer activities.

The Irish Rogue Series begins with *Magic Destiny*. Available in digital and paperback.

www.elizagreenbooks.com/magic-destiny

Get *Rogue Magic* (a free prequel to *Magic Destiny* when you sign up to my mailing list) Check out **www.kategellarbooks.com** for more information.

Ω

TIME WITCH CHRONICLES

(*adult series, adult language, mild romance*)

Looking for a little urban fantasy action? Check out this new series featuring Sylvie and Penley as they navigate the murky past, in this fun, time traveling series.

She's a sassy good witch. He's a death-loving necromancer. Can they stop a murderer from altering their future?

www.elizagreenbooks.com/time-witch

TIME WITCH is available in digital and paperback.

GET IN TOUCH

www.facebook.com/elizagreenbooks
www.instagram.com/elizagreenbooks
Goodreads – search for Eliza Green

Printed in Great Britain
by Amazon